TOMMY WILSON, JUNIOR VETERINARIAN
Book Two

THE CASE OF THE ORPHANED BOBCAT

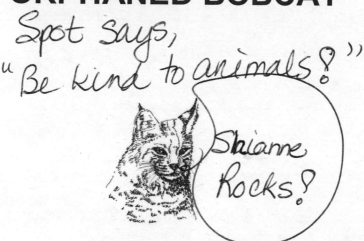

Spot says, "Be kind to animals!"

Shianne Rocks!

Maggie Caldwell Smith

Maggie Caldwell Smith

Published by Magpie Press

Published by
Magpie Press
Post Office Box 6434
Pine Mountain Club, CA 93222

Cover Illustration by Carol Heyer
Bobcat Art by Charlotte White
Refuge Map by Author

ISBN 10 0-9788391-1-0
ISBN 13 978-0-9788391-1-6

TOMMY WILSON, JUNIOR VETERINARIAN
Book Two

THE CASE OF THE ORPHANED BOBCAT

Don't miss the other
Tommy Wilson, Junior Veterinarian
Adventure:
The Case of the Wounded Jack Rabbit

Watch for book three in the series
Due out in fall of 2007

Visit our website:

www.magpiepress.com

To my husband Don,
the wonderful, supportive love of my life,
with whom I am blessed to enjoy
life's adventures.

And to my sister, Suzan, who has consistently
been one of my greatest cheerleaders.

With thanks and acknowledgements to Chuck
Christman for his generosity in inviting me on his
internationally acclaimed Mine Safety and Health
Administration (MSHA) Abandoned Mine Rescue
course; and to the Exotic Feline Breeding
Compound in Rosamond, CA for their wealth of
information about bobcats; to Camille Gavin for her
eagle-eyed perusal and expertise in editing the text;
and to Dr. Diane Cosko, DVM, for her expert
review of the manuscript.

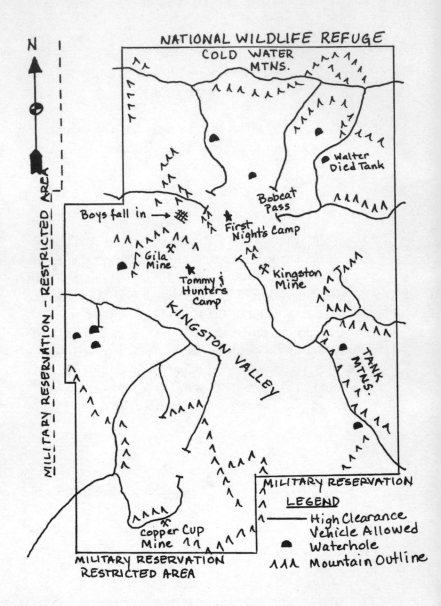

Chapter 1 – A Bobcat Problem

Tommy Wilson grabbed the oxygen tank and wheeled it to the treatment table. His heart was pounding. On the table, an unconscious baby bobcat struggled to breathe, its little, furry chest rising and falling rapidly.

"Hand me another vet pack, would you, Tommy?" Dr. Martinez said, not looking up from drawing blood from the young feline.

Tommy dashed to the glass-paned cabinet and pulled out a pack of surgical implements. He peeled open the blue cloth and laid the tools beside the senior veterinarian.

"Do you think we can save him, Dr. M?" Tommy tried to swallow the lump in his throat. He remembered helping the doctor send a young bobcat to Phoenix last week for autopsy.

"Too soon to tell," the doctor said, using his forearm to wipe the sweat beading on his forehead. "Careful, Tommy, he's unconscious now, but you never know." Tommy tried to steady his trembling hands as he pried open the kitten's jaws so the vet could slide the tube down its throat to help the young feline breathe.

Even though Tommy was only twelve years old, Dr. Martinez trusted him to assist at the Adobe Veterinary Clinic because Tommy had shown his compassion and natural ability in helping animals. Dr. Martinez had been training Tommy for almost a year now.

The doctor examined the lifeless wildcat's eyes and ears and gently pulled back the lips to reveal its gums.

"See here, Tom?" the doctor said, lifting the loose skin on the kitten's body. "He's obviously dehydrated. Look how long it takes the color to return when I press on his gums. There's plenty of water right now on the refuge, so why hasn't he been getting it? And his fever's raging." He showed Tommy the thermometer registering 106 degrees, four full degrees above normal.

"Is it the same problem as the cat last week?" Tommy asked.

"Sure looks like it, but we won't know until some of the tests come back. It's a toxemia of some sort. I don't think it's lead poisoning, or the gums would be blue. We'll send these slides and blood samples up to Phoenix ASAP. Meanwhile, all we can do is treat it symptomatically, with antibiotics, fluids, and isolation."

... and hope he holds on until we get some answers, Tommy silently finished the doctor's unspoken thoughts.

"You want to carry him?"

"Sure!"

"Okay, but watch out for the claws."

Tommy started to wipe his sweaty hands on his smock, but he then remembered he still had on the latex gloves. He could feel his hands stick inside the gloves; the absorbent powder coating was long gone.

The kitten was obviously young, but already the size of a small house cat and weighed more than Tommy expected, nearly ten pounds, he thought. He laid the animal on a fluffy blanket in the intensive care isolation cage where he would be under the watchful eye of a veterinary technician. While the doctor checked the IV line, Tommy gently stroked the soft, lightly spotted fur. His heart leaped as one of the bobcat's small, black-tufted ears twitched.

"You're going to be okay, little guy," Tommy whispered.

"We can also hope Ranger Peterson comes up with some answers on his exploration this week," said Dr. Martinez. "He agreed to track the cats and run some tests on the soil and water."

"Ranger Peterson?" Tommy's heart sank. "But, he's supposed to take four of us ranger interns to the Wildlife Refuge tomorrow."

"I know," said the doctor. "He's planning to have you boys help him with the work. In fact, when we're done here, I have a list of supplies you can pack for the trip."

"Wow, really? How cool. This is going to be great! Maybe we can solve the mystery so no more animals will die."

Later, in the supply room, Tommy laid out half a dozen wrapped instrument sets, a box of latex surgical gloves and two dozen surgical masks. It would be important for the expedition to protect themselves from infection, as well as any possible contaminants.

What was happening to these awesome animals? Tommy wondered. Something was making them horribly sick. This kitten was the second one brought in by rangers. Sadly, Dr. Martinez hadn't been able to save the first one.

His jaw set, Tommy checked the list taped to the cabinet door. He piled the next series of items on the stack: zip-top plastic bags, black permanent markers for labeling, small rubber-stoppered glass vials for collecting samples, and tongue depressors. To these he added several sizes of cat muzzles before collecting the first-aid kit from under the cabinet.

"How's it coming, Tommy?" Dr. Martinez asked as he placed a small neon orange pouch with the supplies. "Tranquilizer darts," he explained. "They're labeled — larger doses for adult cats, smaller for kittens. Only Ranger Peterson uses these, but you know that."

Tommy nodded. The senior veterinarian helped him load the supplies into a nylon duffel bag.

"Peterson is coming by this evening to pick this up. He'll carry it in his own backpack."

"Dr. M, we have to figure out what's hurting these little guys. It's bad enough for them to be killed by predators, but this – this is something different. What can we do?"

"Well, Ranger Peterson will have some ideas, too, but if the problem is a toxemia, then it must be something the bobcats are ingesting – through either their food or water. You'll be testing the water holes and taking spot samples of the vegetation and soil.

"If you can get close enough to any cats," the veterinarian continued, "or any other wildlife for that matter, keep an eye out for any unusual or suspicious behavior. The area you'll be going to holds one of the largest bobcat populations around, so that's where you'll start."

"I just hope we find something that helps, and soon," Tommy muttered grimly.

Chapter Two – The Trip Begins

"Hello, Ranger Peterson," Tommy dropped his pack by the pile of camping equipment beside the Game and Fish Department van. He pulled off his baseball cap and mopped his brow with his T-shirt sleeve.

"Hi, Tommy. Ready for our trip?"

"You bet. I can't wait. This is going to be so neat. A whole week in the desert helping you track and do testing sounds awesome! Best internship class around. Besides, we need to help these bobcats, before any more get sick."

Peterson smiled. "You boys are going to be a big help to me. Actually, you have the most experience, Tommy, so you can be my right-hand man this week, okay?"

"Sure!" Tommy grinned.

"Oh, by the way," Peterson continued, "Jesse Suarez had to cancel so I've replaced him with Hunter Davidson. Hunter's going to be a seventh grader, like you. He just moved here from northern California, so he's new to the desert. He may need a little extra help on the trip."

Tommy's smile sagged. Oh, great. Peterson wanted him to take care of this Hunter kid. He loved helping other people, but this was supposed to be his chance to explore.

Observing the pale and slightly-built Hunter stumble out of his family vehicle as the rest of the boys arrived, Tommy groaned inwardly. This kid would need a lot of extra help. His pack was bigger than he was.

Once all of the participants were present, Peterson announced, "Okay, folks, now's the time for your farewells. We'll take it from here."

"Don't we get to wave goodbye?" asked Hunter's mother.

"You can do all your hugging and waving now. The trip starts with the kids learning to work together. No parental supervision beyond this point."

"Don't worry," said Tommy's father. "The kids are in good hands. Peterson's an experienced outdoorsman and backpacker."

"Besides," the ranger added, "we have a GPS and I'll have my cell phone along in case we get into any difficulties."

"What's a GPS?" Mrs. Davidson asked.

"Global Positioning Satellite," explained Peterson. "It triangulates with satellites so you always know your exact position. Makes it easy for anyone to find you if you need help."

"Well, all right," Mrs. Davidson said, giving Hunter a squeeze. "Your retainer and your regular glasses are in the small front zipper pouch. You took your Dramamine, right? And don't forget to brush your teeth."

Hunter shot his mother a withering look and squirmed uncomfortably, pushing his sunglasses farther up his nose.

Tommy scowled as he heard Matt Beeker whisper behind him, "Oh, this is really going to be great. This kid can't even pack his own gear. He's going to be worse than useless!"

Ranger Peterson shooed the parents away and distributed the remaining food and camping supplies among the boys.

"Wait a minute!" Matt protested. "How come he doesn't have to carry more?" he said, pointing to Hunter.

"Don't worry about it, Beeker," Peterson replied. "Each person has different strengths and abilities that he contributes to the team."

"Okay, but what are his? He's hardly carrying anything extra."

"But, he is carrying something, isn't he? You want to carry it instead?"

"No," Matt answered, looking at his own well-weighted pack. "But it doesn't seem fair."

"Ah, but it is fair," Peterson replied. "Each person's load is appropriate to his weight and experience. That's as it should be."

Ranger Peterson straightened from his task. "Okay, men. I'm glad to have each of you along. We're going to have a great week, as long as we cooperate and work together. Most of my colleagues call me 'Pete'. You can, too."

Dusting off his hands he adjusted his Game and Fish Department ball cap. "At the end of our trip, you'll each get one of our official ranger hats."

"Cool," the boys echoed.

"Everyone's read the desert information sheets I gave you ahead of time, right?" All the boys nodded. "Good. Pile in and let's go! Let's give Hunter first crack at the front seat – let him get a feel for the desert terrain."

"Yeah, we don't want him hurling all over the van!" Andy White said.

"What's the matter, Hunter?" Matt added. "Do you get seasick on the desert?" The two boys snickered.

Tommy sighed. What a bummer. This Hunter kid was going to spoil everything. How in the world did he get invited on the trip?

Chapter Three – The First Night

From his seat by the window behind Ranger Peterson, Tommy watched the miles of neatly groomed farmland flash by. Rows and rows of irrigated green fields evolved into desert sand dotted with creosote and burro bushes.

The ranger was explaining to Hunter, "Even though it's June, spring was late this year and we've had unusually heavy rains. That's why there are still so many blossoms."

Tommy tapped Hunter on the shoulder and pointed to a saguaro cactus not far from the roadway. It stood like a Native American rain dancer, multiple arms raised toward the sky. At the tip of each uplifted arm was a small cluster of individual white and yellow flowers.

"These guys are ancient," Tommy said. "Saguaro don't even start blooming until they're fifty years old!"

"Wow," said Hunter, gaping at the scenery around him.

"Hey, look!" Tommy exclaimed, pointing at a bounding jack rabbit's backside racing away from the van.

"Okay, Mr. Nature Guide," Matt scoffed. "Cool it. We've all seen millions of those."

"Well, maybe Hunter hasn't," Tommy said.

"Oh, yeah, right," Matt said. He cast a glance at Andy sitting next to him and they snickered.

Tommy scowled and leaned forward so he could hear Peterson's commentary to Hunter. The ranger was pointing out the occasional razorback ridges of volcanic rock that rose from the otherwise flat and monotonous terrain.

"Amazing," said Hunter. "How high are they?"

"About three to four thousand feet," said Peterson.

"They look like someone squeezed a glob of dark goo up from the ground," Tommy said, "and then it froze there." The two boys laughed.

After two hours, Ranger Peterson turned the van off the main highway and entered a well-groomed dirt and gravel road at the entrance to the National Wildlife Refuge. Even with the van windows rolled up Tommy could hear the tires crunching over the gravel. The vehicle lurched along the uneven surface stirring up a cloud of dust.

At six p.m. the ranger edged the van off the road into a small clearing surrounded by creosote bushes, broom-like ocotillo and cholla cacti. The vehicle lurched to a stop and the dust settled. After the cool of the van's air conditioning the desert heat felt like the inside of a pizza oven.

"Whoa," exclaimed Hunter. "It's hot!"

"Maybe that's why they call it the desert, moron," said Matt.

"Actually, Matt," corrected the ranger, "a desert is determined more by the amount of rainfall than by the heat. And please don't use that tone with each other."

Matt scowled and wandered away to go to the bathroom in the shelter of a rock.

A few minutes later everyone reconvened at the van. They unloaded their gear and began the hike to their campsite. Along the way, they took a break in the shadow of a rock overhang, snacking on trail mix, juice and water.

When they arrived at their campsite about seven forty-five, Ranger Peterson gave each of the boys a job. Tommy and Hunter unpacked the food and water, while Matt and Andy collected large rocks and built a fire ring.

"Okay, boys," the leader called them together. "Let's put out our bedrolls before it gets too dark. Dinner will be a snap, so let's get settled first. Smooth out a level place for your sleeping bags. Put down your Thermalite mats first and then your bags on top. If your bag isn't water repellent, you'll need one of your big garbage bags over you so you're not soaked by morning. Even though it's dry now, the amount of dew overnight will surprise you."

The group set about making their sleeping arrangements. Tommy unrolled his Thermalite pad and opened the valve, the faint hiss confirming that the tough, lightweight pad was inflating. Using his boot he scraped away some small pebbles and then laid down his pad. On top of this he spread out his sleeping bag. A T-shirt inside his stuff bag served as a pillow.

While Matt and Andy were setting out their beds on the other side of the fire ring, Tommy noticed Hunter fumbling with his insulating pad and other gear. His inexperience was obvious. Tommy decided he'd better help him.

Why did Tommy always have to be the one to help out? He just wanted to focus on solving the mystery of the bobcats on this trip, but he approached the other boy anyway.

"Can I give you a hand, Hunter?"

"I guess so," the newcomer answered. "Thanks." Tommy helped him select a spot and set out his bedding.

Later, with dinner and clean up out of the way, the boys and their group leader talked around the campfire.

"Have you all got your maps?" Peterson asked. As the boys pulled the maps from their packs, the ranger pointed out several probable bobcat dens to the northeast of their camp.

"Tomorrow we'll check out some of the locations and take water samples at the water holes, which are called 'tanks' there on your maps."

"Hey, Pete," said Andy. "This one sounds good – it's called 'Walter Died Tank'." Everyone laughed.

"I c-can't believe how c-cold it is." Hunter's teeth chattered as he talked.

"It's amazing, isn't it?" Peterson agreed. "The temperature can drop thirty degrees as soon as the sun goes down. You'd never have believed it earlier today, but hypothermia can be a problem on the desert."

"Hey, hypothermia – th-that's one of the f-four dangers we read about on those sh-sheets you gave us," Hunter said.

"That's right, Hunter," the ranger said. "You've done your homework."

Hunter beamed through his chattering teeth. He quoted, "The four primary sources of danger for people wanting to survive in the desert are hyperthermia, dehydration, hypothermia, and injuries."

"Teacher's pet," Matt muttered.

"What a geek," Andy agreed.

"Excellent, Hunter," said Peterson. "Hypo means too little, hyper means too much heat. Matt, how do we guard against hyperthermia?"

"Uhm, well, uh – stay out of the sun?"

"Well, that's sort of right," the ranger answered. "We don't have to stay out of the sun all together, but we need to limit our exposure to the direct sun, and drink plenty of fluids. Just like a car's engine overheating, if we ask too much of our body's cooling mechanism, it can break down.

Peterson continued, "Those of you with fair skin and blue eyes – Tommy and Hunter – you need to be even more sure you pour on the sunscreen and keep your sunglasses on."

"What are we going to do for water, Pete?" asked Andy. "I'm almost out already."

"That's good, Andy. That means you've been drinking frequently like you should. Keep your water readily accessible, on your belt and at the top of your packs. We've each had a gallon of water for the first day, but water weighs a lot, so starting tomorrow, we'll be exploring ways to find and 'make' water here in the desert."

"Cool," the boys echoed.

"And, guys, this is really important," the ranger continued. "Like I told you before we left, always use the buddy system. Never go anywhere without checking out and in, and that includes taking a leak. Always tell someone where you are going!"

"If you have to pee during the night," he went on, "get up and do it, then crawl back into your bag as quickly as you can. But don't go very far away. Right behind that rock over there should be fine." He indicated a large rock formation about twenty feet away.

"If you do happen to get lost or separated," the ranger said, "stay where you are and let us find you. That's what the whistles are for. Are you all wearing your whistles?"

All of the boys lifted up the whistle tied on a cord around their necks.

"Good. Now, tonight, the temperature will probably drop to the low sixties. That may not sound very cold, but if your clothes or sleeping bags are damp, it's going to feel really chilly. Everyone's changed out of their sweaty clothes, right?" The boys nodded.

"Keep them inside your packs for tonight. If you leave them out, they're going to get soaked. Tomorrow while we hike, you can drape them over your pack and they'll dry out. They'll provide a change of clothes for tomorrow night. By alternating your clothes each day like this, you will always have dry clothes to put on."

At bedtime when Hunter went off a short distance to go to the bathroom, Tommy noticed Matt and Andy approach him. Tommy couldn't hear the words, but he could see that Hunter was uncomfortable, almost shrinking as the boys talked with him. Suddenly, Hunter stiffened and the discussion became more heated. The newcomer walked quickly back towards the camp, avoiding Tommy's gaze as he passed.

Tommy frowned. What was that all about?

Chapter Four - Missing

In the morning, Tommy could feel the tingle of the crisp desert air as he opened his eyes and poked his head out of his sleeping bag. Peterson was already up and restarting the campfire, setting out some of the food for breakfast. He waved good morning as he saw Tommy stir.

Tommy yawned and stretched and pulled himself out of his sleeping bag. He noticed Hunter's bag was unzipped and there was no sign of the newcomer. He must be an early riser, Tommy thought.

Tapping his boots together upside down to make sure no critters had crawled in overnight, Tommy stuck his feet into them and went over to help with breakfast preparations.

"Sleep okay?" Peterson asked.

"Yeah," Tommy replied. Drawing a deep breath of clean, fresh air, he said, "It's so great out here. I love it!"

"Rise and shine, men!" Peterson called to those still sleeping. "It's seven o'clock, time to get up and at it!" Gradually Matt and Andy roused themselves and showed up at the fire.

"Where's Hunter?" Peterson asked.

"Uh – off going to the bathroom, I suppose," Matt answered. "Maybe he wanted some privacy." He gestured toward the rocks at the base of the mountain. He and Andy exchanged glances.

Peterson frowned. "He's been gone since I got up half an hour ago." He squinted in the direction of the rocks.

"Well, I've got to go, why don't I go look for him?" Matt offered.

"Okay, but take Andy with you – remember our buddy rule. And don't forget the 'leave no trace' rule – pick up any TP you use." The boys grimaced, but took a baggie with them and set off for the base of the mountain a couple hundred yards away.

Tommy watched them as they left. They were talking and gesturing intensely. He could hear them calling for Hunter. While the boys were gone, Tommy helped Peterson get breakfast ready: granola, reconstituted milk, fresh oranges, Tang, and energy bars.

Andy and Matt returned with concerned looks on their faces. They had found no sign of Hunter.

"When was the last time anyone saw him?" the ranger asked, looking at each boy in turn.

"He went to bed when the rest of us did," said Tommy. "I woke up about one-thirty and he was in his sleeping bag."

Matt and Andy exchanged glances again.

Peterson strode to Hunter's bedding. "When he was gone so long, I checked his bag. Looks like he wanted us to think he was there. He put his cap at the head and stuffed his daypack and some gear down inside the bag, to make it look like he was sleeping there. Where could he have gone?"

No one spoke.

"Well," the ranger continued, "let's douse the fire and look for him. I don't want to sound the alarm just yet. He may turn up soon, but he should have known better than to go off alone. That's why I stressed the buddy rule so strongly." He tossed Hunter's cap onto his sleeping bag.

"He couldn't have gotten that far – could he?" Andy asked, sneaking another glance at Matt.

"We don't know how long he's been gone," Peterson answered, "or which direction he went. When we search, we'll go to the top of the mountain and use the whistles and binoculars. I'll put in a call now to the ranger station. If we don't find him by ten o'clock, they'll send out search and rescue. In this climate and terrain, we can't afford to have him lost for long, or his chances of survival are —" he stopped. "Well, we have to find him quickly, that's all."

"Oh, man," Andy groaned. "I knew we

19

shouldn't have done it." He looked miserably at Matt.

"Shut up, stupid!" Matt growled.

"What for?" Andy answered. "Hunter's missing and it's our fault."

"No it's not," Matt said. "We didn't make him get lost. He did that all by himself."

"No he didn't," Andy snapped. "You know he wouldn't have gone if we hadn't dared him."

"What are you boys talking about?" Peterson asked, interrupting the argument.

Reluctantly, Andy began to explain how he and Matt had challenged Hunter to climb to the top of the mountain in the dark to be the first to find a bobcat den. They woke him at midnight and sent him off, then they went back to sleep. It never occurred to them that he wouldn't make it back.

Peterson glared at the two boys. "I can't believe you did that. You know that violates all the rules. What in the world were you thinking?" He threw his own hat down in disgust.

Matt defended their actions. "I mean, you go to the top, you turn around and come back. What's so difficult about that? Only Hunter could get lost doing something that easy!"

"That's no excuse!" Peterson fumed. "It was a stupid thing to do – and now you see why." His jaw was set.

"So, at least now we know when and where he went," the ranger continued. "But we don't know why he didn't come back. Oh, Lord, what if he's gotten hurt?

"Well, we'd better get started. Matt and Andy, I don't want the two of you together. Andy, you go with Tommy. Matt, you're with me. Each of you, get your daypacks ready with all the gear on your list. We'll go up the mountain together and split up when we get to the top. Tommy, you have binoculars, right? Bring them.

"And you all have your whistles, right? Remember the signals: three short blasts, rest, three short blasts, repeated, mean emergency. Three long blasts, repeated, mean all clear. If one of the teams finds Hunter, give the emergency whistle and the other team can come and help. "We'll leave a big note here for Hunter. If he returns, he can give us the all clear signal and we'll come back. Any questions?"

No one had any. Their faces were grim.

Oh, man, Tommy thought, Hunter had to be okay. Tommy felt awful. He could tell something was going on last night. He should have said something. But, now, instead of helping the bobcats like they came to do, they had to spend time looking for Hunter. What a mess.

Chapter Five – The Search

With their daypacks loaded, Ranger Peterson, Tommy, Matt and Andy started up the mountainside in search of Hunter. Loose dirt and gravel made the way treacherous. With the sun beating down on their side of the mountain, the temperature was climbing quickly. When Tommy checked his thermometer it showed ninety-eight degrees.

"Whew, this is farther than it looked," Matt groaned.

"Yes, it is, isn't it?" Peterson said pointedly.

They stopped twice in the shade of rock overhangs, to rest and drink water. After thirty minutes they arrived at the summit of the small mountain peak, winded and sweating.

"Wilson, you start at north on the compass point," the ranger said. "Pan your binoculars slowly all the way around, going counterclockwise. I'll go clockwise."

There was no sign of Hunter, or any other living thing.

Then they divided the area to search on foot. Tommy and Andy went down the back side of the mountain; Peterson and Matt went down the ridge leading off to the southeast. They were to search for thirty minutes and then head back to camp. The ranger showed them how to mark their way with forked sticks and arrows formed from stones on the ground.

Tommy had to bite his tongue to keep from chewing Andy out. What a jerk! Just so he could be a big shot! Yet, Tommy felt partly responsible, too. After all, Ranger Peterson had asked him to look out for Hunter.

The two boys spread a short distance apart to cover more ground. Neither spoke, except to call for Hunter. In the distance Tommy could hear the others calling the missing boy's name.

About twenty-five minutes into their search, Tommy spotted a fragment of red nylon, snagged on a prickly pear cactus. Andy!" he called. "Over here!"

They stooped to inspect the piece of material. Tommy pointed. "It looks like he might have slipped up there. See the skid marks? And maybe he caught his jacket on the prickly pear. He must be around here somewhere," he said excitedly.

"But we don't know for sure that it's Hunter's jacket," Andy said. "It could have been here for a long time."

"No, it would be more faded. This looks new, like Hunter's." He glared at Andy. "All of his equipment is new, because he's never been camping before."

Tommy was surprised at his own boldness, but he was angry at how the boys had treated Hunter.

Andy squirmed. "Well, I still say there's no way we can tell it's his. Besides," he said checking his watch, "it's time to head back to camp."

"We can't quit now," Tommy argued. "We're so close. He could be around here somewhere." He stood and yelled, "Hun-ter!" He cupped his hands, "Hun-ter!"

"But Pete said we should head back at eight forty-five," the other boy insisted.

"Oh, so now you're going to do what Pete says?" Tommy challenged. "When it's convenient?"

"Now, wait a minute! We had no way of knowing Hunter would get lost. We just thought it was a funny joke."

"Oh, yeah, real funny. He could die out here because of you!"

"Well, then, all the more reason we should do what Pete says and head back."

"But Hunter's been missing for hours already," Tommy argued. "We can't leave him out here any longer."

"We need to go back."

"We need to keep looking." Tommy stood with his fists clenched by his sides.

The boys stared at each other. It was a stand off.

"Okay, tell you what," Tommy suggested, "I'll stay here and look for more clues. That way we'll know the exact spot. You go back to the top and signal the others to come over here. We won't really be splitting up, because we'll be able to see each other the whole time."

Andy agreed and started back to the crest of the ridge.

Tommy watched him for a few minutes, and then turned back to his task. He stooped to inspect the spot more closely where Hunter appeared to have slipped. He could see what looked like the indentations of two shoes and a backside, skidding down the slope for several feet. Yes, Hunter had been there. He knew it.

He rose and carefully studied the area all around him, trying to detect which direction the boy had gone. There were no other clues. He continued slowly down the slope scanning to his right and left. Pausing, he glanced up the hill behind him. Andy was almost to the top.

Tommy watched his searching partner reach the crest about four hundred yards above him. There Andy stopped and looked around. He whistled through his fingers, waved his arms and shouted.

He turned to Tommy and called, "I'm going down to the camp to get them. I'll be back."

Tommy waved an acknowledgement and continued his search. Loosening the bandana around his neck, he mopped his brow. After a long gulp of water he returned the bottle to his belt and proceeded down the steep slope.

Where in the world could Hunter be? If he'd gotten lost or disoriented during the night, he should have just sat down and waited until daylight. By now he would have to know he was on the wrong side of the mountain.

But if Hunter was here, why couldn't Tommy see him anywhere? It wasn't as though there were lots of places to hide. That was part of the danger of the desert – the absence of shelter.

What was that sound? More animal than human. He paused, listened. Hunter? No, it sounded like a kitten, crying. A baby bobcat? Had he found a bobcat den?

He crept closer, eyes searching, ears straining to hear. Careful, he told himself, frightened animals could attack, and mother wildcats would ferociously protect their young. Tommy peered around the uphill side of a large boulder. Nothing.

Squatting, he crawled closer. Maybe down the hill a bit? Wait! Was there an opening? A bush was blocking his view. He inched forward. Yes, there was a hole. He didn't see it until he was almost on top of it. Oh, no, what if Hunter had fallen in there? With a bobcat? Yikes!

Tommy lay on his stomach and edged forward until he reached the hole in the ground. His heart was thumping in his chest. He could see it was the opening to a mineshaft, opening into a huge cavern below him. The distance to the bottom made him dizzy. How far was it? Thirty feet? Forty?

He strained to see. Was there something down there, hidden in the shadows? He couldn't tell. But much closer, only a few feet below him, there was a beam sticking out from the wall of the shaft. On it crouched a bobcat kitten, crying.

Tommy's heart tugged – the innocent little face looked up at him, pleadingly.

"Oh, wow!" Tommy exclaimed. "You're kind of stuck, aren't you, little guy?"

He had to help, but what could he do? What if the kitten tried to jump and got hurt? How far away was it? Any sudden move might spook the stranded animal. Moving as little as possible, Tommy eased out of his daypack and felt for his work gloves. Slipping them on, he stretched out his arm. It was too far away. He couldn't reach it. The kitten shrank in fright.

"Okay, okay, little one, don't move. You just stay right there. Let me go get some help."

Tommy shifted his weight to get up, when all at once he felt the ground give way beneath him.

He let out a yell.

He was falling, falling. It felt like he'd done a high dive off the thirty-foot platform at the pool. He grabbed for the beam, but couldn't hold on. The momentum spun him around the beam like a gymnast. He had a vague sense of something soft as his gloved hands scrabbled for the beam. Then came a wailing snarl from his feline companion.

He was still falling, but at least his feet were beneath him now. The mass of fur was clutching Tommy's head like a fur hat. He could feel the claws digging into his scalp. The bobcat was screaming, too.

Then, the falling ended and he landed with a jolt. He grunted as the wind was knocked out of him.

He had tried to let his knees absorb the shock, but still he felt it all the way up his spine. The uneven ground pitched him to his right and he rolled, over and over, the kitten now in his arms wailing.

He finally stopped rolling and lay still, but the world kept spinning. Then, everything went dark.

Chapter Six – The Dungeon

Tommy was awake, more or less. What in the world had happened? Where was he?

He groaned and tried to sit up. Every bone in his body hurt. Was anything broken? He wouldn't know until he moved. He tentatively tried each limb – first one arm, then the other, then each leg. He was relieved to find everything worked all right.

He was lying partially on his right side amid some sort of debris and dirt that had landed on top of him. But, what was that lump under him?

Oh, no! The kitten. His own pain forgotten, he rolled over and felt for the animal.

There was no sound from the baby bobcat. Oh, it had to be okay. He couldn't forgive himself if he had hurt this poor little creature.

In the semi-dark of his dungeon he could see the bobcat's tiny, spotted chest rise and fall. It was breathing, barely. What a relief.

Tommy grunted as he sat up. Dust and debris fell off him. Now that he was up close, he could really see the wildcat. It was younger than the one at the clinic, at most maybe ten to twelve weeks old. Even though it was a little larger than a regular kitten, it seemed awfully thin. How much did it weigh? Maybe five pounds?

Tommy had to know how badly the kitten was hurt. Was it sick like the others, or just thirsty from being stranded in the mineshaft? Or worse, badly injured from this fall? If it came to, it might bolt or attack. It was only a kitten, but it was still a wild animal.

His jacket was in his pack. He could cover the baby bob and protect both of them that way. But where was his pack? He craned his neck to look. Super, it was part of the stuff that had landed on top of him.

Trying not to startle the kitten he eased his daypack around so he could unzip it. There, he had it. Out came his fleece-lined windbreaker.

Tommy gingerly scooped up the baby wildcat in his jacket. The feline sneezed and wheezed, spluttering out some of the dust it had inhaled when they fell down the shaft.

"Easy, little guy," Tommy murmured. "You're going to be okay now. Tommy's here and he's going to help you. Don't you worry."

But in his own heart, he was worried. He must have fallen into an abandoned mine shaft.

There was a small ring of light coming from the hole above, but everything else around him was in shadow. It was at least thirty feet up to the top. How in the world was he going to get out?

The kitten struggled and whimpered. Was it in pain? As he held the baby bob close and rocked it, stroking behind its ears, he could feel the animal relax.

"See?" Tommy said. "I'm going to take care of you. You'll see. We'll get out of here." He only wished he believed it himself. He fought back a shudder.

Wait! What was that sound? What else was down here? A cold-hot chill ran down his spine as he strained to see into the shadows.

There it was again. A moan?

"It's about time somebody got here," mumbled a disembodied voice.

Tommy was incredulous. "Hunter?" he said.

"Who is it?" the other boy said. "Tommy? Boy, am I glad to see you."

Cradling the kitten in one arm, Tommy scrambled several feet over to where Hunter lay. The light of the shaft still illuminated a spot on the floor, but now they were in the shadows.

"You've been down here since last night?" Tommy asked. "Are you hurt?"

"Well, yeah," Hunter replied. "I think my leg's – I think it might be broken." He rested his head on his arm. It was awful."

"I can imagine. But, don't worry. Pete and the others are looking for us. I guess we do need to signal them, though."

He pulled his whistle from inside his shirt. "Did you use your whistle last night?"

"Oh, man," Hunter groaned. "I left it at the camp. It kept getting in my way, so I took it off to sleep."

Tommy put his whistle to his lips and blew a shrill blast.

Hunter screamed, clapping his hands over his ears as the loud noise reverberated in their enclosed space. The bobcat hissed and struggled inside Tommy's jacket.

Tommy moaned. "It really echoes down here."

"Yeah, but does it reach the surface?"

"Guess we won't know until we try," Tommy said, grimacing as he blew the emergency signal.

Hunter buried his head in his arms and plugged his ears while Tommy blew the series of blasts. Then he pleaded, "Stop! I can't take any more."

"We might as well wait a few minutes and then try again," Tommy said. "If they can hear us, they'll signal back. Meanwhile, let's see what we can do to help you. Is it just your leg?"

"Just my leg?" Hunter said sarcastically.

"Well, you know, I mean is anything else broken?"

"I don't know," Hunter whispered. "I've

been afraid to move much. It hurts too badly." His voice cracked.

"Gosh, Hunter. Maybe I can help. But what about this kitten?" he said more to himself.

"What kitten?" Hunter said.

"There was a bobcat kitten trapped on that beam up there. He fell down when I did."

"So that's what it was. I could hear it crying but I thought I was delirious."

"Maybe I can find something over here to hold the baby bob so I can help you."

Tommy glanced around their underground dungeon, straining to see in the dim light. They were in a sort of horseshoe-shaped cavern. Tommy guessed it to be about twenty feet across, with a ceiling of nearly six feet. The shaft above them was about five feet across, narrowing near the top. It led to the surface thirty feet above, where the opening was partly blocked by a bush.

Tommy scouted in the cavern among the leftover mining supplies. "Hey, here's an old wooden crate. Says 'explosives' on it, but it's empty. That'll work for now."

"Mm-hm," mumbled Hunter. "Can you find my glasses? They came off when I fell."

Tommy gently set the kitten down and placed the crate over it and then felt around for Hunter's glasses.

"Here they are," Tommy said. "They look okay." He held them up to the light to inspect them, then handed them to Hunter.

"Thanks. Gosh, it's good to be able to see again."

"So, tell me where you're hurt."

"I already told you," Hunter snapped. "My leg."

"Okay, okay. What part of your leg, and which one?"

"My left one." Hunter grunted as he tried to move. "Right there, above the ankle. Can you tell if it's broken?"

Pulling off his work gloves, Tommy gently probed Hunter's leg. It was quite swollen. He squeezed a spot above the ankle.

Hunter screamed. "Stop!"

"Sorry. Can't tell if it's broken without x-rays, but at least it's not a compound fracture."

"Oh, great. So, the bone's not sticking out. I feel better," Hunter muttered testily. "It really hurts." His voice cracked again.

"Yeah, I'm sure it does," Tommy agreed. "I think we should splint it."

"Splint it?" Hunter echoed.

"Yeah, I saw some boards over here. They look like a kind of plywood. They should work." He dragged a couple of short planks over to Hunter. "Hmm, they're too long. Let me see if I can break one."

He held the board down with his foot and pulled sharply. The rotten plank snapped jaggedly. "Super!" Tommy said. "We're in business. Okay, here goes."

"Okay," Hunter said, leaning back on his hands and squinting his glasses up further up on his on nose. He shifted gingerly.

Tommy put the boards along either side of Hunter's lower leg. He rummaged in the small zipper pouch of his backpack for some duct tape.

"Hey, careful!" Hunter yelped. "Don't move it so much!"

"Oh, sorry, but I've got to wrap the tape all the way around."

"Well, okay, but please be careful. It really hurts."

"I know. I'm sorry." Tommy could tell Hunter was trying to be brave, but no matter how he tried he couldn't stifle the moan.

"I think something for the pain might be a good idea," Tommy suggested. "And some water and an energy bar."

"You have all that with you?"

"Me? Sure, never go anywhere without a first aid kit. And I packed my daypack like Pete told us, plenty of survival supplies."

"Water! I'm dying of thirst. I had my water bottle, and a granola bar in my pocket, but those are long gone."

Munching on an energy bar after gulping down great swallows of water and two ibuprofen, Hunter mumbled through the food in his mouth, "It's just so good having someone else here. I – I thought I was dead for sure." He choked back a sob.

"Yeah, must have been pretty creepy, being down here all alone and hurt."

"It was so dark." Hunter shuddered.

"You didn't have any light?"

"No, it was pitch-black. Matt and Andy —" Hunter left the sentence unfinished.

"What, Matt and Andy wouldn't let you bring your flashlight?"

"How did you know?"

"When you turned up missing this morning, they finally admitted what they had done. That's when we set out to look for you. Those creeps."

"I can't believe I fell for it. Pretty stupid, huh? Anyway," Hunter continued, "it was night time and the moon went behind the clouds and it was totally dark, so I didn't see the opening. I think the fall must have knocked me out for awhile. Once I woke up, I yelled and yelled, but no one could hear me." He took another long gulp of water. "How did you get here?" he asked Tommy.

"Andy and I were on this side of the mountain looking for you. I found a piece of your jacket snagged on a prickly pear, so I knew you had to be around here. It never occurred to me, though, that you'd be underground."

"Well, I didn't see the hole because of the dark. What's your excuse?"

"I heard the kitten crying. When I finally found the hole to the shaft, it was mostly covered by that bush up there, I lay down and looked in. The kitten was stranded on that beam. When I tried to get up to go for help, the ground caved in under me."

"Maybe that's what the planks are from," said Hunter, "an old cover over the shaft. The boards seem pretty rotten."

"Yeah, must be." Tommy squinted up at the surface. "But right now we need to think about signaling the others again, and then take care of this poor baby bobcat. If you can handle moving a little, you might be more comfortable leaning against this mound of dirt. It looks like it might have come from a cave-in."

"Good idea," Hunter agreed.

Tommy helped Hunter struggle to a sitting position using the mound to prop himself up. Glancing around their dungeon, he said, "If we weren't stranded this would be a pretty cool place. I love exploring."

One side of the cavern was bounded by the large mound of rocks and dirt that reached almost to the ceiling. Two other sides of the cavern were sheer dirt and rock face, apparently dug or blasted out by miners. The final side was like the open end of a horseshoe, with two man-made passageways leading further into the mountain, at about forty-five-degree angles.

Narrow rail lines ran into the cavern from each of the two side tunnels, converging into a turnstile about fifteen feet from where Hunter lay. Against the far side of the cavern near one of the tunnel entrances, still on the tracks, was a rusty ore car.

Hunter's voice snapped him back to reality.

"Tommy, how are we going to get out of here?" Hunter whined, squinting up the shaft. He groaned as he shifted his weight. "What if they can't hear us? What are we going to do?" He squinted his glasses further up on his nose.

"Of course they'll find us," Tommy answered. "Andy will be back with the others any time now. It won't be that hard for them to find where Andy and I split up. And, from there to the mine shaft is only a few hundred feet."

Tommy blew several more cycles on the whistle and then rested. "Guess that's all we can do for now, isn't it?"

"Yeah," Hunter sighed, leaning back against the mound and closing his eyes.

His leg must really hurt, Tommy thought.

Tommy had been lucky in his fall. He remembered how he felt when he broke his arm last year – it was awful. He didn't know how Hunter made it through the night, all alone and in such pain. Matt and Andy deserved to be hurt, not Hunter. Hunter was just the victim, poor guy.

Except now Tommy was stuck trying to take care of Hunter and himself and this bobcat baby instead of investigating what was poisoning the bobcat population, the real reason they had come on this trip.

Chapter Seven – Near Escape

Tommy stooped and peered through the slats of the crate holding the kitten.

"Now, let's see what we can do for you, little guy," he said.

"Is he hurt?" Hunter asked, eyeing the young bobcat suspiciously. "Will he bite?"

"Yes, I'm sure he can bite," Tommy said, slipping on his work gloves again. "Right now he's still stunned from our fall. I don't know yet if he's hurt. I sure hope not or I'll feel even worse."

With his windbreaker in hand, he lifted the crate and snatched the baby wildcat. Stroking the animal tenderly, he waited until it settled down a bit. He could feel it purring. Then he peeled back the edges of his jacket to inspect it. The little face with the big round eyes stared up at him.

Tommy's heart melted. "You are so cute," he exclaimed. He sat with the bobcat in his lap, holding the nape of its neck with his left hand, feeling its body with his right. Grappling with his heavy work gloves, he tenderly probed the kitten's neck, shoulders, ribs, hips, legs. When he reached the right foreleg, the kitten yowled and pulled away.

"Okay, little one. Looks like we found something, didn't we?" He tried again to probe the leg.

The kitten gave a throaty growl in protest.

"What is it?" asked Hunter.

"It's this right foreleg, but he won't let me touch it. Must be pretty sore."

"Poor little guy," Hunter agreed. "What can we do for him?"

"He's got to be dying of thirst," Tommy said. "I wonder how long he was trapped. He's so skinny and he's dehydrated. See how his skin's so loose?" he said as he pulled up the skin on the kitten's other foreleg. "How can we give him a drink?"

Tommy scanned the cavern for anything helpful.

"Wait!" he exclaimed. "I have some carrots in my pack. We can empty them out and use the plastic baggie."

"Great idea," Hunter said.

Tommy pulled the plastic zipper bag from his pack and dumped the carrots in his lap. Pouring a small amount of water from his bottle into the bag, he held it for the kitten to drink. It sniffed, then took a tentative lick, then drank more and more, drinking desperately until the water was gone. Tommy grinned at Hunter, who was smiling broadly.

"That's cool," Hunter said.

"Yeah." Tommy nodded. "I love taking care of animals." He paused. "Now let's see what we can do about his leg. Hey, we can do a little splint on it. There are some tongue depressors in my first aid kit."

He searched in the red nylon pouch. It took him only a few seconds to find the tongue depressors and some self-sticking elastic "vet wrap". With his knife he cut a piece of the elastic wrap about six inches long.

"Now what?" Hunter asked.

"You hold him. Keep him inside my jacket so he doesn't scratch you or get away. Hold tight, but don't squash him. Here, you use the gloves. I can't splint him with these on, anyway. There are some surgical gloves in here, too. I'll use those."

Tommy gently handed the kitten, still wrapped in his red windbreaker, to Hunter. Gathering the loose carrots, he slipped them into the small pouch in his backpack.

"He won't bite me will he?" Hunter asked.

"Well, keep your hands behind him and hold him firmly inside the jacket. He'll probably squirm when I try to splint his leg, but don't let him go."

Hunter's teeth were clenched and he was breathing fast. Tommy swiped the back of his hand across his forehead and took a deep breath.

He pulled on the surgical gloves and gathered the depressors. Talking quietly to the baby bobcat, Tommy felt the right forearm. The animal hissed and fought when Tommy touched a spot just above the paw.

"Okay, okay, little guy. I know this hurts," he said grimly, "but it's going to feel better when we're done."

Holding his breath, Tommy placed one of the flat sticks under the forearm. The kitten squirmed.

"Hold him, Hunter."

When Tommy put the second depressor on the top of the arm, the bobcat began to writhe frantically, slipping from Hunter's grasp.

"Hunter! Don't let him go!"

The kitten wailed and began to scramble free from the jacket. Tommy lunged for the escaping animal and caught him one-handed by the fur on the back of his neck. As the kitten lashed out, its claws slashed Tommy's other forearm.

Tommy yelped. The pain in his arm seared all the way up to his shoulder, but he held on to the animal.

Panting, he held up the kitten with his left hand as he pushed himself to a sitting position. Hunter was moaning and holding his injured leg.

Snatching the windbreaker from Hunter's lap, Tommy supported the rest of the bobcat's body with his other hand.

"Hunter, you've got the gloves on. Grab him here behind the neck!"

"But, my leg," Hunter whined.

"Hunter, help!"

Still moaning, Hunter warily grasped the nape of the kitten's neck.

"Hold on. Don't let him go," Tommy said. Blood was trickling down his right forearm. It stung like crazy.

Hunter moaned. "My leg. Sorry. I couldn't hold him."

"It's okay," Tommy reassured. "It happens to the pros, too. I should have had you hold him this way to start with. My mistake. I'm just glad he didn't get away." He shook his arm to relieve the sting.

"So," Tommy continued, "let's try this again." He grinned. "Keep your left hand there while I wrap him in the jacket again. Then hold his body with your other hand and I think we can get this done."

Hunter held the kitten securely while Tommy wrapped the jacket around it. This time Tommy managed to secure the leg between the two tongue depressors and bind it with the vet wrap.

"Now," Tommy said, "we need to keep him safe and relatively immobile."

"You think the crate's too small?"

"Yes, only because he needs a place to go to the bathroom, but we can't have him running away and getting lost." His thoughts were formulating. "How would it be if we lay the crate on its side and use some boards to build a little pen?"

"Sounds good," Hunter said.

Tommy laid the crate on its side, with the open end against the dirt mound. Then he laid a plank over the gap so the kitten couldn't escape. He weighted the plank down with a stone.

"Don't put it too close to me," Hunter said, squirming.

"Don't worry, he won't get out."

Taking the kitten from Hunter Tommy placed him inside his new little "den." He watched with a grin as the baby bob hobbled to inspect his new home, sniffing in every corner.

"What are we going to call him?" asked Hunter.

Tommy considered. "How about – Spot?" he suggested, peering at the kitten's fluffy, lightly spotted fur.

"Yeah, that fits," Hunter said with a smile. "I like it."

"Spot it is, then," Tommy said.

"Guess we'd better fix your arm," Hunter said. "Rinse it first, right?"

"Yes, I hate to use any of the water, but cat scratches are prone to infection, so we'd better wash it. There's a tube of antibacterial soap in the first aid kit, and some more surgical gloves."

Hunter pulled out the gloves, soap and ointment, along with a gauze pad and surgical tape. After helping Tommy wash the three-inch long scratch, he applied the ointment and then taped the gauze in place.

"Hey, you're pretty good at that," Tommy said.

"Well, it is kind of an interest of mine. A lot of kids think I'm a nerd, but I like science. I want to be a doctor, maybe even a specialist in cancer research."

"Cool. I want to be a veterinarian."

"So I've heard. Sounds like you've already got a lot of experience at the clinic. You must be pretty smart."

"Nah, I'm really not very brilliant. I just love animals and when I enjoy something, I don't mind studying and working hard. I'll bet you're smart, though. You get good grades?"

"Well, yeah, but sometimes I'm a little weak on the, you know, the practical side. I've got a lot in my head, but I haven't used it much."

"Yeah," Tommy muttered grimly. "Looks like we're both going to be getting a lot of practical experience."

Chapter Eight - Whistling

"We'd better signal again," Tommy said. "Plug your ears."

The young bobcat wailed loudly as Tommy blew several cycles on the whistle. As the shrill echoes died away, Tommy plopped down beside Hunter.

"They must have heard that," Tommy said. "They can't be far away now." He was trying to reassure himself as much as Hunter. As the boys sat in silence, Hunter closed his eyes to rest.

Tommy couldn't stand having nothing to do. "This is going to drive me nuts," he muttered to himself. Maybe he could scout around the cavern a little.

Maybe there would be something interesting or useful among the mining supplies on the other side of the cave. Stepping over the narrow rail lines, he peered into the rusty ore car still resting on the rails.

An old lantern creaked as Tommy lifted it by its rusty handle. Blowing dust and soot off it, he coughed as some bounced back in his face. He shook the lantern gently and held it up to the light. Still a little fuel in there. What would happen if he lit it? He'd try it later, when Hunter was awake. For now, he carefully set the lantern at the base of the dirt mound behind him.

What else was there? An old Thermos container, the short and round kind families used on picnics. It seemed relatively modern, but who could have left it there? It wouldn't hold a lot, about two gallons, but enough for a couple of days. With effort he unscrewed the lid, grunting as years of dust and dirt resisted, but eventually the top came off.

Pew! Rancid air escaped. He coughed, almost retched, fanning the air to clear the odor. Otherwise, the Thermos was intact. If they could clean it, it might be useful. Disinfectant pills should do the trick.

The only problem was, there was no water. Both he and Hunter were surviving off of Tommy's two partial water bottles. At least they weren't in the scorching sun. In fact, they had the opposite problem – hypothermia, like Pete had said. The mine was cold and damp. Good thing they both had jackets. He shivered. Maybe he should put on his jacket and long pants.

Setting the Thermos beside the lantern, Tommy shrugged on his jacket gingerly over his bandaged arm and rummaged in his pack, pulling out his lined, red nylon pants. He unzipped the cuffs and slipped them on over his boots, then returned to the ore car.

He found lots of dirt and rubble, but nothing more inside the car. Stepping past it he peered deeper into the shadows. Was there something over in the corner? He inched closer. It was too dark to tell. He could get his flashlight, but they needed to be sparing with it. It had to last – who knew how long.

Curiosity got the better of him. He had to know what it was. Retrieving his flashlight, he shone it in the corner. Something black and yellow, half buried in the rubble, round with something sticking out on top. What was it?

He stepped closer and gingerly poked at it with his boot. A miner's hard hat, with a light on top. Way cool! Did the light work? Probably not after rusting down here for years, but it was neat, even so. He stooped to pick it up, tipping it to let the dirt to fall. Out came a dead bat.

With a start, he dropped the helmet and jumped back. He loved animals, but bats were not his favorite, especially dead ones. Still, the helmet was neat, so he kicked it again, then picked it up. It looked okay. Dusting it off, he set it by the other rescued items. It would be fun to fiddle with later.

Hunter stirred and sat up, yawning. "Gosh, it's almost noon," he observed, checking his watch.

"I'm surprised they haven't found us yet. You didn't hear anyone, did you?"

"No, now that you mention it, I didn't. I was exploring over here in these old supplies and kind of lost track of time."

"But, Tommy, how can they find us if we're not signaling?" Hunter whined.

"I'm sorry, Hunter." Tommy sighed. "But why do I feel like the bad guy here? This whole thing isn't my fault, you know. We were supposed to be out here helping the bobcats, but we had to stop to look for you – and now we're both stuck down here."

"Well, I – uh, uh –" Hunter sagged against the mound of dirt. Suddenly, he burst into tears.

"It's all my fault," he wailed. "This is all my fault! I got us into this mess, and now no one's going to rescue us. And we're going to die down here. And it's all my fault." He sobbed uncontrollably.

"Gee, Hunter, take it easy," Tommy said. "It's okay. I mean, we'll keep trying. It's not too late. They're bound to find us soon."

But, honestly Tommy did feel like it was all Hunter's fault. No, actually, more like Matt's and Andy's fault. If they hadn't tried to prove they were big shots, none of this would have happened.

Hunter's sobs died down. He sniffed. "You think so? Gosh, I mean, I don't know how much longer I can stay down here. But, at least it's daylight now, and you're here. That really helps."

Drying his eyes, he said, "Sorry, guess I sort of lost it there."

"I'm sorry, too," Tommy said. "It's really not your fault. Matt and Andy are jerks. But you're right. We do need to keep signaling and I should have been doing that."

"Maybe we should signal every five or ten minutes or something. You know, set our stopwatches and signal regularly. That would be a good idea, wouldn't it?"

"Yes," Tommy agreed. "That is a good idea."

"And we can do it in shifts," Hunter said.

"Okay, but I'll take the first shift. It's been a while already, so I'll blow three cycles now, then wait ten minutes and do it again, and so on. You rest."

"It's a deal," Hunter sighed and lay back against the mound and closed his eyes, pulling his jacket tighter around him.

Between whistle signals, Tommy busied himself by collecting materials in the cavern. Behind the ore car, he found two shovels, a large pickaxe and a small one, a few rotten wooden beams, some newer plywood planks, and a lot of rocks and rubble. In the area directly beneath the shaft opening, he made a small fire ring outlined by boulders which he found in the rubble.

Every ten minutes, he stopped, looked up the mineshaft and blew two cycles of the signal, accompanied by wailing from Spot. Nothing. Where was everybody?

Chapter Nine – Cloudburst

Almost an hour later, Hunter stirred again. "Pretty neat," he said through a yawn, looking at the scene before him.

Tommy grinned sheepishly. "I had to keep busy or I was going to go nuts. I know smoke is one of the best ways to signal, so I made the fire ring. We'll probably want it for the heat, too, if we, uh, you know, need to stay down here tonight." He cleared his throat.

"Still no sign of anyone, huh?"

"Nah." Tommy dusted off his hands. "I've been blowing the whistle every ten minutes and nothing. I can't figure out why they haven't found us. I mean, Andy should have been able to show them where we split up – but of course, Andy didn't believe it was your jacket I found, so maybe he didn't even bring them back over here. He probably thought I was going to give up and head back to the camp. Anyway, by now, I'm sure Pete has called in Search and Rescue, so they'll all be looking. But, they should be able to hear the whistle, shouldn't they?"

"I sure hope so," Hunter said. "But we really don't know how far up the shaft the whistle carries, do we? Maybe they can't hear it on top, even if they are there."

"Yeah, maybe not. That's why I was thinking of the fire, but we really don't have much to burn, you know? Just these boards, and there are a few pieces of broken beams that must have fallen in the cave-in. But, there's not much in the way of kindling, and I'm not sure we really want to burn the boards anyway. What if we need them for something else?"

"Like more splints," Hunter groaned.

"Or whatever. By the way, how's your leg?"

"A little better," Hunter answered. "The splint really does help, and I'm sure the ibuprofen did, too. I can't believe I actually slept through all your whistle signals –" he stopped and looked doubtfully at Tommy.

"Yes, I did signal every ten minutes. And, yes, you did sleep through all of it. But, pain takes a lot out of you."

"Yeah, I know." Hunter's shoulders sagged as he leaned against the mound.

Tommy squinted up the mineshaft at dark clouds racing by his telescopic view of the world.

"Looks like a storm is brewing," he said. "I've been seeing more and more clouds."

"Yikes!" Hunter yelped as a brilliant flash of lightning ripped across the sky. Brief seconds later came the resultant explosion of thunder.

"Oh great," Tommy moaned. "The storm is here!"

No sooner were the words out of his mouth than the sound of heavy rain pounded the earth above their heads. Large drops fell down the narrow shaft, splattering on the dirt floor of their cavern.

"How long do you think the storm will last?" Hunter asked.

"There's no way to tell. Sometimes they're really quick, like over in a few minutes, or sometimes they go on for hours."

"Oh, great," Hunter moaned. "Will they still be searching for us?"

"I don't know." Tommy sighed. "The planes will be grounded, for sure. I don't know about ground crews. With the lightning this close, they probably have to seek shelter, too."

Both boys watched glumly as the thunder and lightning played a gruesome symphony above their heads. Torrents of water continued to fall. A wail from Spot caught Tommy's attention.

"He must be afraid of thunder," Tommy said. Pulling off his jacket, he lifted the lid on Spot's cage and snatched him behind the neck before he could bolt. Plopping down on the mound, he wrapped the kitten in his jacket and rocked him gently. Somehow, it was comforting to Tommy to hold the little feline and soothe him. "There, there, little guy. It's going to be okay. Don't worry."

The heavy rain turned to a deluge. There was a waterfall of muddy water tumbling down the shaft into their cavern. Where was it all coming from?

Tommy gasped as the realization hit him. "We're getting the run-off from the mountain. It's washing downhill and falling into the mineshaft. Hunter!" he cried. "Hurry! We have to save the supplies before it's too late."

With Spot in one arm, Tommy snatched the kitten's crate and scrambled to the top of the mound, out of the reach of the falling water. He turned the crate over and set it on top of Spot, who was now wailing loudly.

"Sorry, little guy. We've got to take care of these things. You'll be safe there."

From the bottom of the mound, Hunter handed Tommy his backpack and their various tools. Tommy set them on the side of the dirt mound out of the way of the water. He scrambled over and rescued the lantern, the Thermos and the hard hat. Next came the wood. They saved as much as they could, but the rain pelted on. The boys were drenched and water was starting to fill the bottom of their cavern. Hunter, still lying on the floor, was stranded in water that was slowly rising.

Tommy extended his hand to Hunter. "Come on. We have to get you out of that water." He grunted as he pulled Hunter onto the side of the mound. The boys lay there panting, watching the water slowly inch up the stones around their signal fire ring. They wouldn't be lighting a fire there any time soon.

Hunter closed his eyes and lay back, moaning. The sudden movement to save the supplies and get out of the water obviously hadn't helped his leg.

The cloudburst ended almost as suddenly as it had started, but heavy rain and wind continued for several hours. The boys looked dejectedly at the pool of water below them.

"Now what are we going to do?" Hunter asked. "If we can't build a fire there's no way to signal anyone. No one will ever know we're here." He didn't say more, but Tommy already knew his thoughts: we're going to die down here.

"No, we're not," Tommy insisted, answering Hunter's unspoken conclusion. "There has to be a way out of this. We just have to find it. What are our options?" He slid down the mound and waded through the calf-deep water. Squinting up the mineshaft, he flinched as a raindrop hit him in the eye.

Just then, there was a rumble. The boys stared wide-eyed at each other as their cavern shook. Tommy jumped back to the mound as mud, water and debris tumbled even faster into their underground dungeon, large clumps of it hanging-up on the beams in the shaft.

Less and less light entered their cavern. Was the storm building again? With a great crash a huge boulder from above slid over the opening to their mineshaft and everything was pitch-black.

———

Chapter Ten – Buried Alive

In the darkness of their dungeon, Hunter cried out, "Tommy?"

"I – I'm right here."

"What – what happened? Why's it so dark?"

"I don't know," Tommy answered slowly.

The total darkness was almost suffocating.

"Was it an earthquake?" asked Hunter.

"I don't think so." Then he realized what had caused the sudden darkness. "It was a mudslide. The cloudburst caused a flash flood that brought down part of the mountain. I think a big rock closed off the shaft."

"We've been buried alive!" Hunter shrieked. "Oh, I knew it. I just knew it. We're going to die down here!"

"Hunter, please. Try to calm down."

"It's the dark. I hate the dark."

Tommy shuddered. "Yeah, me too, but we have to try to keep it together."

"I'll t-try," Hunter stammered, teeth chattering.

"Where's my backpack?" Tommy groped in the dark for the nylon bag. There it was. Going strictly by feel, he unzipped the main pouch and felt for his flashlight. It wasn't there. A cold chill ran down his spine.

He groaned. Where could it be? He had used it to check out the materials in the cavern. Where had he put it? Oh, man, he could hear his father's voice, "Always put things back where they belong. You never know when you'll need to find them."

"Hunter, have you seen my flashlight? I had it out before the storm."

"It's here somewhere. I know I handed it to you."

"You're sure?"

"Yes, I handed it to you with the pickaxes, or sometime in there."

"Okay." Tommy exhaled carefully, trying to steady his nerves. "It's got to be here, then." He felt systematically for it. What if it rolled back down the mound into the water? They really needed the light. Wait! He had the butane lighter. If it wasn't too wet, it might work.

He fished in his shorts pocket, inside his nylon long pants, for the lighter.

"Yay!" he exclaimed as the flame sputtered

and lit. "It's not much, but it sure beats pitch-black."

"Boy, I'll say," said Hunter.

With the aid of the lighter, Tommy found his flashlight among the supplies. It still worked. But they had to be really sparing with it now. Except for the little lighter, it was their only source of light.

Choking back a sniffle Hunter said, "So now what do we do? It's obvious no one will find the mineshaft now."

"Yeah, that's for sure," Tommy agreed. He was silent a moment. "What are our other options?"

"Well, if we can't go up, I guess we need to go – out?" Hunter ended his suggestion tentatively.

"I agree. The tunnels have to go somewhere. I think we should figure out what all we have to work with and then decide on a plan of action."

"Okay," Hunter agreed. "Why don't I hold the flashlight and you sort the stuff."

"Deal. Okay, we've got the leftover mining supplies: two shovels, two pickaxes, a hardhat with light, but we don't know yet if the light works, a smelly old Thermos jug, plus some now very wet wood." Tommy put all the mining supplies in one area atop the mound.

"Shine the light on my pack here," Tommy said. "Most of what I have is in it." He proceeded to pull everything out of his daypack.

The two boys sorted the items from Tommy's daypack: food in one pile, survival aids in another, clothing in another.

Clothing, there wasn't much. They were already wearing just about everything. There was an extra neon orange bandana and an extra pair of socks. They might come in handy somehow.

Surveying the pile of survival supplies, Hunter said, "I can't believe you got all this stuff into your daypack."

Tommy grinned. "I guess I'm a good Boy Scout. I like to be prepared. My dad says I improvise as I go along."

"Neat," said Hunter, sorting through the items. "We've got a broken mirror, a heavy-duty plastic garbage bag, a sewing kit. It even has safety pins. Matches and a butane lighter, a spiral notebook, 30 feet of nylon rope, and a small roll of duct tape."

"Wait until you see the first aid kit," Tommy said proudly. He opened the bright red water-tight nylon stuff sack to show its contents, naming some of the items as he pulled them out. "Band-Aids in all sizes, moleskin for blisters, sterile gauze bandages, antiseptic swabs, the antibacterial soap and antibacterial ointment, and a single-use ice pack. There's even this little plastic bottle of distilled water."

He rummaged through more items in the kit. "And here's the ibuprofen, Benadryl tablets, sunscreen, insect repellent, Solar Edge, eye drops, iodine pills for sterilizing water, protective latex gloves, tweezers and Q-Tips, and an elastic bandage. It all stays really neat in this pouch. Cool, huh?"

Hunter nodded. "I just hope we don't need all these things."

"No joke. Okay, all the food's in this pile," Tommy said.

It wasn't a very big pile. Most of the two quarts of water were already gone. Four of his original eight granola bars remained and he still had two apples and most of the carrots. A zip-top bag of turkey jerky and a bag of trail mix had not yet been consumed. Three packets of string cheese and two small boxes of crackers were also still unopened.

"What's in here?" asked Hunter, holding up a plastic bag containing red powdered granules.

"Strawberry Gatorade. It keeps your electrolytes in balance, and it tastes better than iodine pills."

"I've never had iodine pills, but I'm sure strawberry Gatorade is better." Hunter grimaced.

To the supplies Hunter added the few items he had in his pockets: a tube of sunblock Chapstick, gritty with sand, a small tube of antibiotic ointment, a wad of string about five feet long, antihistamine tablets, Dramamine tablets, a small bottle of Tylenol, a small tube of sunblock, moisture-producing gum and several gum wrappers, a pocket knife, a comb, a wallet with ID, a water-logged map of the Wildlife Refuge, and sixty-five cents in change.

Tommy's Swiss Army knife, a gift for his twelfth birthday in April, was almost a survival kit in itself. He now pulled it out of his pocket to add it to their survival supplies.

He was glad it was dark so Hunter couldn't see him blinking back the tears as he tenderly fingered the smooth surface of the knife. He felt his throat tighten and his eyes sting when he thought of his parents who had given it to him. He cleared his throat and swallowed, trying to move the lump.

What if he never saw them again? They had been so excited to give him this gift he wanted so badly. And now – he would give it up in a second if that could take him back to his family.

"Wow! That knife is really cool," said Hunter, squinting at it in the beam of the flashlight. "It's got all sorts of gadgets, huh?"

"Yeah, it is pretty slick," Tommy said. "It's the super deluxe model. My mom and dad gave it to me for my birthday," he said as his voice cracked. He leaned forward to show Hunter some of the functions of the knife, demonstrating the blades, the different screwdrivers, the pliers, wood saw, chisel and fish scaler.

"There's even a toothpick and a pen," he finished, handing the knife to Hunter.

"Too cool," Hunter repeated, inspecting the bottle and can openers, the scissors, the magnifying glass and the corkscrew. "We won't be opening any wine bottles, but maybe this will come in handy for something."

"Yeah." Tommy couldn't hide his discouragement. "Too bad it can't dig us out of here."

"No lie," Hunter agreed. "Hey, what's in that extra pouch?"

"This has a compass and thermometer, needle and thread and a bunch of other stuff."

"Man, it's freezing down here! What does the thermometer say?"

"It's about sixty-five degrees." Tommy squinted at the plastic instrument.

Hunter shivered. "Wish we could light a fire."

"I know," Tommy said, "but with no hole up above, it would only get smoky. Besides, the wood's too wet to burn."

"The lantern!" both boys shouted in unison. They laughed. It was the first time either of them had smiled in several hours. Tommy scrambled to the lantern and dragged it back to where they both sat. Hunter shone the flashlight as Tommy wiped off the glass globe.

"I'm sure there's fuel in it," Tommy said. He carefully lifted the glass and laid it beside him. "I think you twist this thing up, and then light it. My dad has one of these in the barn. It was my grandfather's."

Tommy struck a match and held it to the fabric wick. Nothing happened. He held it until the match almost burned his fingers.

"Why won't it light?" He frowned.

"Maybe it's just dusty," Hunter offered, and blew on it.

"Hey!" Tommy coughed as the dust blew into his face.

"Oh, sorry."

Tommy laughed. "That's okay. It probably is really dusty." They both blew again on the wick and Tommy flicked it with his finger. He cranked the wick up a little farther and shook the lantern. He could hear liquid sloshing.

Striking another match, he held it to the wick, which finally caught, smoldering at first. Then, there was a small flame.

"All right!" both boys shouted, and gave each other a high-five. Tommy carefully slid the glass cover back onto the lantern and turned the wick up a little.

"Yay!" Hunter shouted. "We have light. What a relief."

The whole atmosphere in their dungeon lifted with the presence of the light. It was almost cheery.

Hunter drew a deep breath. "You know, I'm starved. Seeing all this food makes me hungry. Should we have some lunch?"

"Good idea," Tommy said.

For lunch each boy had a package of string cheese, a box of crackers and a few baby carrots. They finished what was left in one of the two quart water bottles, leaving the other half bottle for the next day.

"Spot's got to be dying of hunger, too," Tommy said. "I wonder what he'll eat." He held up a bit of his cheese to the kitten. Spot sniffed at it and mewed at Tommy. "Go ahead, little guy. Try it. Sorry, but it's all we've got. Not as good as mama's milk, but maybe it'll do in a pinch."

Obviously ravenous, the kitten reconsidered. After a tentative lick, it snatched the cheese from Tommy's fingers and swallowed it in one gulp.

"Okay!" Tommy said. "Here, try a little more." He grinned at Hunter as Spot consumed the cheese. "Guess we lost the bag from the carrots," he said. "What else can we use?"

"How about the hardhat?" Hunter suggested.

"Great idea!" said Tommy. He shook out the hat, turned it upside down and poured a little water into it. Carefully lifting the edge of Spot's crate, he set the water inside. Spot sniffed warily, then lapped at the water. Tommy was pleased.

"We need to find another way to let Spot out of his cage to go to the bathroom," Tommy said. "Hmm, maybe a leash of some sort."

"Good idea," said Hunter. "How about we use some of this nylon rope?"

"Yes, we can do it without cutting it, in case we need it later. We can just tie this end around his neck and unravel what we need. That way we can keep him from running off."

With a bit of struggle, the boys put Spot on the leash and let him hobble around on the dirt mound. Then they returned him to his crate for safekeeping.

"Tommy, these lights aren't going to last forever. We're buried down here, remember? What are we going to do?"

"Oh, yeah," Tommy snapped back to reality. "I think the tunnels are our only option." The blue-green luminous dial on his watch indicated it was nearly four-thirty p.m. "It's been a really long day," he said. "Maybe we should wait until tomorrow to start."

"You're probably right. And I'm afraid you're going to have to do the exploring." Hunter ruefully tapped his splinted leg. "What am I going to do while you're gone?"

"I wonder if you could use one of these shovels as a cane? It would give you some mobility, for when we find the way out."

"That might work," Hunter agreed. "Let me see one." He slid down the mound with a shovel in hand. Tommy shone the light while Hunter practiced.

After trying awkwardly for several minutes to walk with the shovel, Hunter landed in a heap in the muddy water at the bottom of their cavern. When he did so, Tommy got an idea.

"Hey, Hunter!" he cried. "Look – look at all the water we have!" He gestured at the pool of water Hunter was lying in.

"Very funny," the other boy growled, picking himself up from the pond. "That hurt," he groaned.

"No, I'm serious. Look, we have all this water. All we have to do is collect it and purify it and we can drink it. We won't die of thirst, anyway!"

"Oh, well, that's comforting." Hunter grimaced as he wrung water from his clothing.

"But we need to collect it. What can we

store it in?" "Come on, Hunter, think!" He wanted Hunter to come up with the idea.

Grudgingly Hunter looked around. "Well, there's that old Thermos."

"Great idea! I'll rinse it out a few times and fill it with water. We can use my iodine pills to purify it."

"You have your tablets with you?"

"Sure, they're in the first aid kit, remember?"

"Oh, yeah. I guess I figured we didn't have enough water for it to matter."

"Well, we do! Let's get busy."

"Okay, okay," Hunter said, actually smiling, sitting gingerly on the side of the mound and scooting back up the hill.

Tommy carried the broken vacuum jug to the water puddle and rinsed it several times. Then he gently tipped it and let it fill slowly with water from the top.

"We'll have to let it stand for a while for the dirt to settle," Hunter said.

"Yeah, then we can transfer it to our water bottles and purify it."

"Wish I still had my bottle," Hunter muttered.

"What happened to it?"

"It was down here somewhere. I used it last night. Gosh, was that just last night? Seems like forever ago. Anyway, it was empty so I didn't think I'd need it anymore. I got so frustrated being stranded down here, I threw it as far as I could. Guess I've done some pretty dumb things so far."

"Yeah, well maybe between the two of us we'll have one good brain."

"You have such great ideas," Hunter said enviously.

"I'll bet you have good ideas, too, Hunter. You just never let them get very far. You shoot them down before they've seen the light of day."

Hunter stared at Tommy. "You think so?"

"Yes, I do. From now on, I want you to say your ideas – no matter how stupid you think they are. Deal?"

"Okay, deal."

The boys sat in silence for several moments.

"Tommy?" Hunter asked. "Are you okay?"

"Yeah, just thinking – about my family and our farm and about the animals I rescued a few weeks ago. When we get out of here, I want to show you the Animal Clinic. I think you'll really like it. And, I have an awesome fort I built in a dry canal near our farm. I'll take you there sometime."

"Yeah, sure." Hunter's voice sounded hollow.

"Come on, now," Tommy urged. "We're going to get out of this. We have to keep believing."

Hunter didn't say anything.

Tommy thought, what if Hunter was right and they were going to die down there? Please, no, God, he thought. They had too much to live for. Their families needed them and Hunter still had so much to experience in the desert. No, there was too much to live for. They just couldn't give up yet.

Tommy was almost afraid to suggest what he knew needed to be done. Hunter wasn't going to like it.

"Hunter?"

"Yeah?"

"We probably need to turn out the lantern so we don't use all the fuel."

"Yeah. I knew it was coming. Well," Hunter said looking at his watch, "I guess we should try to get some sleep anyway, right?"

"Right." Looking at his own watch, Tommy was startled. "Gosh, it's already nineteen forty-five, seven forty-five p.m.!"

"So you use military time, too, huh?"

"Yes, my dad taught it to me. And the rangers use it, too. I think it's kind of neat. For any time after noon, you start adding the hours to twelve, so there's no way to mix up a.m. and p.m. You always know exactly what time you're talking about."

"Yeah, pretty cool."

"I think I might be able to go to sleep," Tommy mumbled through a yawn. "How are you doing? Need something more for the pain?"

"Some more ibuprofen might be a good idea. And maybe I should sleep up there on the top of the mound. My leg hurts more when it's hanging down."

"Sure," Tommy agreed.

After helping Hunter get settled and then carving out a place for himself on one side of the mound, Tommy extinguished the lantern. He drifted into a restless sleep, dreaming about his family and farm.

Tommy spent a fitful night. He wasn't sure exactly when he first woke up. He dozed again, and the next time he awoke, his watch read one-thirty in the morning. Man, would this night never end? It seemed so long – and cold – and lonely, even with Hunter there.

Suddenly, Tommy was wide awake. What was that? He saw the flashlight bobbing.

"Hunter?"

Hunter gasped. "Oh, you're awake. You scared me. I was looking for some more ibuprofen. My leg's really hurting."

"Let me get it."

"Thanks," Hunter mumbled as Tommy handed him the tablets and some water.

"Long night, huh?" Tommy said.

"Not as long as last night. It really helps having you here. I don't think I could do another one alone."

"I usually don't mind being alone, but this would be stretching it."

Hunter didn't answer. Tommy could hear his soft snoring. Good, he thought. He really needs to sleep. Tommy drifted off to sleep again, too.

Chapter Eleven – Explorations

Tommy heard Hunter yawn.

"What time is it?" Hunter asked.

"Seven a.m. Oh-seven hundred hours." Tommy said.

"I guess that makes it morning," said Hunter, "not that there's any way to tell in this darkness."

"Yeah. Time for me to get started. I know the others are looking for us, but they'll never find us here. We've got to do something to get out of here."

"I wish I could go with you," Hunter whined. "Please don't leave me alone down here."

"Hunter, you know you're in no shape. First, I need to find the way out, then we'll go together."

"But what if you get lost? I'll die down here."

"If I get lost," Tommy muttered grimly, "we'll both die down here. I'll be back in a few hours. While I'm gone, why don't you let Spot out for a walk, but don't let him get loose. Maybe you can purify more water and repack our supplies. Once we find the way out, we're not going to want to stick around!"

"Okay," Hunter sighed, but Tommy could tell he was unhappy.

"Look," Tommy reasoned, "I can work much faster on my own, because I'm not injured. We'll both get out that much sooner."

"I know," Hunter said. "I just, well – "

"I'm scared too, but we can't let that keep us immobile – or we will die down here."

"You don't act scared at all."

"You said it. I don't 'act' scared. I just cover it well, which isn't always a good thing. Underneath I'm scared, too."

After a breakfast of carrots and strawberry Gatorade, the boys weighed the pros and cons. They decided Tommy would explore one tunnel at a time. One of the two tunnels seemed to slope downhill because the water from their cavern appeared to be flowing in that direction.

The boys consulted the map of the refuge Hunter had in his pocket. It had gotten wet, but if they were careful with it, it might last. They were fairly certain they had their approximate location on the map.

Either tunnel could lead through the small mountain range near which their group had camped. Which would lead to an external exit sooner was a toss-up, if either actually would. There was a chance they might just run into another cave-in, but the boys felt they had to try.

They agreed on a marking system and an emergency signal with the whistles. If Tommy came to a fork, he would continue along the original tunnel and mark his route. He would take the notebook and draw a map of the tunnels as he went.

They set a time of one hour. If Tommy hadn't reached an exit by then, he would turn around and come back.

The tunnels had to lead somewhere, Tommy reasoned. With the rail lines, he hoped they would lead to the surface, not deeper into the mine.

He took the flashlight and the extra batteries, the map, the notepad and the pen and started off. It was oh-eight-thirty, eight-thirty Monday morning.

As he started off down the tunnel, Tommy was deep in thought. A lot had happened since they left Hidden Wells on Saturday afternoon. Up on the surface, he knew, others were searching for them. By now there were search and rescue teams, probably helicopters and all-terrain vehicles, but they'd never find Tommy and Hunter down here. Tommy hadn't wanted to say anything to Hunter, but after that cloudburst and flash flood, the searchers would find no clues to Tommy's and Hunter's location. Any snagged jacket pieces, footprints or other evidence were gone forever.

Eventually, the searchers would investigate all the mine tunnels, but that could take a really long time. Tommy had to find a way out.

He was glad he was the one doing the exploring, not Hunter. It would be horrible to have to lie there and wait. Besides, he wasn't sure Hunter could have handled it. But, then, was he sure he could handle it? It seemed to be up to him. If he got lost, they would both die down here.

Why did he have to be saddled with this Hunter kid? He could be doing what they really came to do – helping the bobcats – instead of trying to find their way out of abandoned mine tunnels. Any other time, the exploring would be really cool, but now – their lives and the life of the kitten depended on it. It wasn't fun anymore.

Around and around Tommy's thoughts churned. He had to make himself concentrate. If he made a mistake, even a slight misjudgment, it could cost them their lives. He had to stay focused. He fought down his rising sense of panic. He wasn't particularly fond of the dark either, but he had to keep going. His little flashlight beam didn't feel like much company.

The tunnel was black and cold, with a damp and musty smell. Even though he was moving, the chill seemed to penetrate to his very bones. The floor was muddy because of the run-off from their cavern. Most of the water stayed between the narrow rail lines, so Tommy walked on the outside of the rails. He paused a moment to begin his drawings. It wouldn't do to get lost right away.

On one page of the notebook, he drew a rough sketch of their cavern, the caved-in dirt mound, the turnstile and the rails leading off into the two tunnels. He put a numeral one beside the tunnel he was exploring first. Then, he drew an arrow in the direction he was going.

Not much more to do but trudge on. As he went Tommy shone the light above and to the sides. Nothing but barren rock and dirt walls supported by heavy wooden beams. What must it have been like to be a miner in these tunnels? He didn't think he would have wanted to do it. The constant dark and cold would have depressed him. Even now, he had to fight to keep his spirits up, to keep moving forward.

His path was leading gradually downhill. Soon he came to a tunnel that cut off to his right. He stopped to draw it on his diagram. Knowing the iron in the mountain was probably skewing his compass, Tommy ignored the instrument and just consulted the map of the refuge. If their starting point was correct – that was a big if, but it was all they had to go on – then the new tunnel only went deeper into the mountain. He was glad. That made it less tempting to pursue it.

How long had it been since he left the cavern? It didn't seem he was making any kind of progress. If he hadn't found anything by the end of an hour he was supposed to go back. But, then he'd only have to start all over and cover all this ground again. It was slow going in the dark. Although his flashlight was strong, it illuminated only a few yards down the tunnel. He had to be careful. He couldn't afford to get hurt.

Almost an hour into his exploration, he paused. This was useless. What if it wasn't leading anywhere? It all seemed so hopeless. He could be down here forever, trying this tunnel and that. Without a detailed map of the tunnels, there was no way to know which way to go. But he and Hunter didn't have forever – a few days at the most.

Yet, just thinking about Hunter and Spot, knowing others were depending on him helped him stay focused. With this his determination resurged. He had to get out of here – he had to see his family, and he and Dr. Martinez had more animals to save!

On he trudged, step after step into the darkness before him. Another tunnel led off to the left, but it had no rail lines, so he felt certain it wouldn't lead to the surface. He drew it on his map anyway and kept going.

What was that ahead? His flashlight beam shone on a wall. Tommy picked up his pace until he came face to face with a solid dirt wall. The tunnel and the rail lines ended there. That was it.

Now what?

Tommy wasn't sure whether he was disappointed or relieved. In a way, this door was closed. That helped the indecision, but it closed the door on one possibility. Now they were left with only one other tunnel. What if it, too, led nowhere? He shivered as a chill ran through his body.

Well, back to the cavern. It was the only

thing to do at this point. His time was more than up anyway.

It felt more comfortable to cover a path he'd already taken, but now he was bored. It seemed to take forever to get back to the cavern where Hunter and Spot were waiting. At last his flashlight beam opened into their cavern. What a relief. Strange, that their dungeon felt almost safe.

Chapter Twelve – More Explorations

Hunter awoke as Tommy emerged from the tunnel. His face was hopeful.

"No go," Tommy said with a heavy sigh, plopping down on the dirt mound. "It goes downhill all right, but it just goes deeper underground, or into the mountain. I'm not sure which. Anyway, it doesn't lead out."

"How far did you go?"

"'Til it dead-ended." Tommy tried to put some hopefulness into his words, more than he felt. "There were a few other tunnels, but one had no tracks so I didn't think it would lead anywhere. The other looked like it only went deeper into the mountain. So, I just kept going on in the main tunnel. Then, bam – brick wall – well, okay, dirt wall, same difference."

"It didn't go any farther?"

"Nope. It just ended right there.

"That means the other tunnel is all we have left."

"Exactly." Shining his light around their supplies, he noticed Hunter had been busy. All the odds and ends were packed into Tommy's daypack, and the mining supplies were neatly stacked.

"Hey, good job, Hunter. Now all I need to do is find the way out."

Hunter's voice was subdued. "I'm just so relieved you're back. Gosh, it was awful to be here alone again. I used the lantern just long enough to do this, and then I put it out. Man, that was hard to do. You have to leave again?"

Tommy glanced at his watch. It was almost twelve o'clock, so he had been gone more than three hours. No wonder he was tired. He wanted to start on the next tunnel right away, but what if it led nowhere? He didn't really want to have to face the loss of all their options.

It was so frustrating being totally cut off from the world above their heads. What was the weather like? What was Ranger Peterson doing to find them?

"Hunter – we have to do something. Let me have something to eat and then I'll take off again."

"Okay."

"I know it's hard to just lie here and wait. It would drive me crazy. But, the sooner we find the way out, the sooner we have a chance of getting rescued."

Hunter's shoulders drooped. "I know. You really think we will – find the way out, I mean?"

"Yes, I do." Tommy summoned all the optimism he could find. "We can't give up hope yet, Hunter."

"Right. Well, for lunch, I suggest jerky, more carrots, Gatorade, and I think you should have a granola bar. You're doing all the work."

"Yeah, I am pretty hungry. That was a lot of walking. How's Spot doing?"

"Fine, I guess. I gave him some more water. He didn't like the taste of the iodine very much, so I put a little Gatorade in it. He liked that a little better. I gave him part of a stick of jerky. They're carnivores, right? He wasn't sure about it at first, but then he gobbled it down."

"Great," Tommy said with a grin. "Maybe you should be a vet, too."

"I'll stick to people," Hunter said. "I'm not as good with animals as you are."

After preparing their lunch, the boys extinguished the flashlight and ate in darkness.

"Man, I've never liked the dark," Hunter said, "but now I'm really going to hate it. This is so creepy."

"I'll say. It's weird sitting in total darkness. I've never been anywhere this black before."

"Me either. And I don't ever want to be again!"

"Well, look at it this way. If you've been through this and survived, anything else will be a piece of cake."

The boys chuckled.

"You're always so upbeat, Tommy. I wish I could be that way."

"Some of it's natural for me, I guess, but there are times when I have to decide to be optimistic."

"I'd probably get there eventually, too. You just get there faster."

"But you get there. That's the point. We're just different in some ways, but you have your abilities and talents you bring to the situation."

"Like what? I'm the one who got us into this mess, remember?" He sighed. "I guess I'm used to having people not believe in me, like my dad, especially. He always finds something wrong, no matter what I do. And my mom, she does everything for me, so it makes me feel like I must be brainless, or something."

"You're not brainless," Tommy said. "In fact, we've already established that you're pretty smart. Remember?"

"Yeah," Hunter said doubtfully. "Yeah," he said a little more confidently.

Even in the pitch black Tommy could sense Hunter sitting up straighter. He smiled. This kid might be okay, after all.

"So," Hunter said, "you're going to check out the other tunnel next?"

"Yep. Better get going." Tommy traded his almost empty water bottle for the full one, updated his diagram to include the dead-end, and collected his equipment.

He knew the flashlight was going to fade soon, but he decided not to say anything. He didn't want to worry Hunter any more than necessary. He did have the extra batteries in his pocket, but he hoped he wouldn't have to use them. Having them in reserve gave him a certain sense of comfort.

It was almost thirteen-hundred hours, or almost one p.m. when he started off on the second tunnel. What would this one bring? No way to find out without trying.

Chapter Thirteen – Troubled Light

The flashlight beam seemed a little stronger now, probably from being turned off for a while. Soon, though, it started to fade again. Tommy shook it and tapped it against his thigh. He had to get as much out of these batteries as he could.

He shone the light on the walls and ceiling and floor. This tunnel was pretty much like the other one, about six feet across and ten feet high, and it had the same musty smell. The rails were less rusty, though, which seemed hopeful. There was almost no water in this tunnel, so he walked in the middle of the rails, stepping from cross-tie to cross-tie.

"Drat," Tommy muttered, shaking the

flashlight. The beam was fading fast, but he was determined to go until the batteries totally gave out.

About forty-five minutes into his hour-long foray, the beam was so puny he could barely see a foot in front of him. He didn't notice a broken tie until it was too late.

Tommy yelped as he plunged headlong. With no time to roll to absorb the shock he grunted as he landed flat-out, sprawled between the rails. The flashlight flew out of his hand and went clattering down the track. The faint beam went out almost immediately.

With the wind knocked out of him he groaned, unable to catch his breath from the jolt. He felt he would suffocate before he could get a breath. Forcing himself to exhale, he then managed to draw in a tiny bit of air, then a little more. He lay there panting, trying not to think about the throbbing pain in his left hand.

Oh no, he groaned. This was all they needed. Plus, he had no idea where the flashlight was or if it would work again, even with new batteries. He knew it was ahead of him somewhere. With time he thought he could find it, but this was slowing down his exploring and their chance for escape.

It hurt to move. Two bad falls in two days – maybe nothing was broken, but he was awfully stiff and sore. This was way worse than any baseball practice.

Grunting, he climbed to his knees, unable to stifle a moan as he tried to put weight on his left hand. He growled through clenched teeth. What a stupid move. He should have replaced the batteries sooner.

Pulling himself together, he felt around for the missing light. It was slow going, crawling on two knees and one good hand, reaching out for the instrument with his bad hand. He made a sweeping motion, praying he wouldn't accidentally skip over the light. How far could it have bounced?

He didn't know how long it took before he felt something. Because his injured hand was so sore, it was hard to tell what he had found. Struggling to balance on his knees, he felt the object with his good hand. The flashlight! Now, if only it would work. Please, oh, please! he prayed.

He twisted to sit on his backside, cradling the instrument in his left arm. He found that the plastic barrel was intact, well, almost. He could hear it crackle as he squeezed it. The plastic lens cover over the front was gone, probably popped out when the face smashed. But, the bulb seemed intact.

Holding his breath, he switched on the light. Nothing. He groaned and shook it very gently. Something inside rattled and it wasn't the batteries. The noise came from inside the face, by the bulb and the metal reflecting ring. It was difficult working in the dark, with only one hand.

Then he remembered his butane lighter! It might give him enough light to work. He groped in his pocket for the lighter. Flicking the flint, he sighed as a small flame flickered. By the faint light, he could see that the flashlight was badly dented and bent.

Biting back a groan he grasped the lighter with his injured left hand. When he peered into the flashlight, he could see the bulb. Gripping the light between his knees, he struggled to twist off the head so he could pry out the reflector and the bulb.

The bulb was loose. If the connection was ruined, they were in trouble. He wished Hunter were there to hold the parts, but Hunter was almost an hour back down the black tunnel, and without light, it was going to take Tommy a really long time to get there. He carefully tightened the bulb.

His left hand hurt even more from holding the butane lighter, but he managed to check the batteries and inspect the contact. If he could just get it going enough to get himself back to the cavern, then he and Hunter could work on it together. Maybe they could duct tape it together.

It took him several tries to get the threads to catch, but finally it was screwing down. He closed his eyes and said a silent prayer before he pressed the switch.

Light! He had light! It had worked and a weak beam shone from the flashlight. Tommy would have jumped around the tunnel if he'd been standing, but he didn't want to drop the light. With a deep sense of relief he let the lighter go out. The outside case was hot from burning so long and he hoped it wouldn't burn his pocket. Struggling to his feet, he headed back toward the cavern and Hunter.

"This trip was a waste," he muttered to himself.

Boy, Hunter was going to let him have it. He felt just awful. So much depended on him and then he had to go and blow it like this. He was glad the trip back seemed to take a long time. He didn't feel like hurrying.

When he got to the cavern, he could see the hopeful look on Hunter's face. That made it even harder to tell him what had happened, but Tommy didn't suppose he could hide it. The flashlight was a mess, and his hand needed attention.

Unable to hide his disappointment, Tommy recounted his misadventure to Hunter.

"Oh, wow. Are you okay?" the other boy asked.

"Yeah, I'm fine. Just banged up my hand a bit." It was the first time he'd really looked at his hand. It was already swollen and starting to discolor. "Oh, great," he muttered.

"Gosh, we do have an icepack in the first aid kit, don't we?" Hunter asked. "We need to ice that down before we wrap it."

"Yeah," Tommy said without enthusiasm.

"Look at the flashlight," Hunter said with awe as he took it from Tommy's hand. "I'm surprised it still works."

"It didn't at first. That's part of what took me so long. I had to fiddle with it a bit. I think we'd better tape it back together. At least the jolt gave the batteries some new life."

Tommy yelped as Hunter inspected his

hand. Hunter found the cold pack in the first aid kit, squished it around to activate it, and placed it on Tommy's hand. "We can use the elastic bandage to wrap it in a little while," he said.

Tommy sat forlornly on the mound staring into the dim light of the damaged flashlight. "Aren't you going to yell at me for blowing it so badly?" he asked.

"What good would that do?" Hunter replied. "It's not like you did it intentionally. You were trying to do the right thing. Besides," he added looking down at his splinted leg, "I don't think I could have done any better." He smiled.

"Well, thanks," said Tommy. He managed a smile, too. But, inwardly he wanted to cry. They had to find a way out of the tunnels, and it was still up to him. What if he couldn't do it?

Chapter Fourteen – Another Night

B y the time the boys were done bandaging Tommy's injured hand, it was nearly seventeen hundred hours, five in the evening, though it was impossible to know that from external cues. Their dungeon was still totally black, except for the light of the lantern.

They decided to take a break for dinner and discuss their strategy. The meal was meager, consisting of trail mix, jerky and carrots. Since Tommy had done most of the work, Hunter insisted that he eat one of the remaining granola bars. To one bottle of the purified water, they added a small amount of Gatorade, which helped disguise the taste.

At least there was some enjoyment having Spot with them in the cavern. The boys let him wander the mound on his leash for a while. Tommy wished he could play with him, but he couldn't risk the kitten's getting away. Besides, if they were going to release him into the wild, they shouldn't tame him too much.

Tommy grinned as he fed Spot a little jerky. The kitten took the food willingly. Tommy offered a piece of the granola bar, but Spot was reluctant about it. Eventually he ate it, obviously ravenous.

"Should we call it quits for the night?" Hunter asked.

"I don't know." Tommy shrugged. "Without the lantern, it's pitch black, so who can tell whether it's day or night? We could work around the clock."

"Yeah, but you'll get too tired. That's when mistakes happen. I think it's better to get some sleep, then get a fresh start tomorrow morning."

"You're probably right. I am tired." He hung his head.

Smoothing out their sleeping spots again, they extinguished the lantern. As they lay in the total darkness, Hunter spoke.

"I met your mom and dad and sister in the parking lot. Do you have any more in your family?"

"No, we're it. I mean, we have a farm and some animals, so they seem a part of the family too, you know what I mean? But, I only have one sister. Emily's almost eight. You have any brothers or sisters?"

"No, there's just me. Guess my parents have kind of spoiled me a bit, being an only child and all."

"What does your dad do?" Tommy asked.

"He's a civil engineer. He's going to be working on some of the bridge and highway renovations in the area. My mom's a nurse, so she just started at the Wellness Clinic."

"Neat," Tommy said.

"Does your mom work on the farm, too?"

"Yeah. She handles some of the business stuff. We're part of a co-op, a cooperative, so we rotate crops with the other growers and my mom helps with the sales and distribution of the products."

"What kinds of stuff do you grow?"

"We have alfalfa, mainly used as hay for livestock. We have corn, both for human consumption and for fodder, and tomatoes."

"Cool. Do you ever help on the farm?"

"Yeah, especially during harvest times, but we do have three full-time employees, plus seasonal workers. My folks know I really want to work with animals, so as much as possible they let me work at the vet hospital."

"Your parents sound super."

"Yeah, they are." Tommy tried to swallow the lump in his throat.

He hoped it wouldn't hurt Hunter's feelings, but he was too tired to listen any more. He drifted into a fitful sleep. His hand throbbed and he had nightmares about wandering forever down endless tunnels and trying to put things together without having all the parts.

Hunter, too, was restless most of the night. Tommy heard him get more ibuprofen during the night, but didn't check his watch for the time. This night also seemed endless – cold, dark, dismal. Tommy pulled his jacket more tightly around him and tried to get comfortable, made difficult by the pain in his hand.

Tommy awoke with a start. The darkness was like a heavy blanket smothering him. He fought down the sense of panic, forcing himself to breathe slowly. Inhale, exhale, inhale, exhale. He must have slept again, for when he checked his watch it read oh-five-thirty – five-thirty in the morning. That meant it was Tuesday morning, the start of their third day in the cavern.

Enough, he thought. Time to start getting ready for more explorations. He felt for his flashlight and switched it on. Thank God, it still worked. He fumbled in his pocket for the fresh batteries and put them in. He couldn't risk a repeat of yesterday.

Hunter woke as Tommy stirred and sat up.

"How'd you sleep," Tommy asked.

"A little better than last night. You?"

"Kind of restless. Can't wait to get going."

After their small breakfast of the remaining two granola bars and the other bottle of Gatorade, Tommy collected his supplies and started off down the second tunnel. It was a little after six in the morning. Today he had to make some progress. He just had to. Their food was running out, and the total darkness was almost making him crazy. If they didn't get out of the tunnels soon – well, he didn't finish that thought.

Hunter agreed to purify the last of the water remaining in the thermos and to feed and let Spot out of his cage while Tommy was gone. He was also going to practice using the shovel as a crutch.

Chapter Fifteen – More Choices

This morning the tunnel was the same as it had been yesterday. A jagged rock stuck out of the wall at one point, and when Tommy passed it he knew he wasn't far from the broken cross-tie he had tripped over.

He slowed his pace and watched the ground for the hazard. There it was. He came to a full stop, shone the light beyond it and then carefully stepped over the broken tie. Today it had only taken him thirty-five minutes to cover the same distance. From now on he had to proceed more slowly again because the ground was unfamiliar.

A few steps beyond the broken tie, he had to make a choice. Two tunnels led off, one on each side. They both had rail lines. Now what? Well, he had to do what they had agreed on. He drew the tunnels on his diagram, including the rails, and the broken tie in the main tunnel, and then moved on.

He was tired – and hungry, and his hand throbbed. Struggling to maintain hope, he kept going. How much farther, he wondered? He couldn't think about that. It almost made him panic. All he could do was investigate the tunnels.

Another forty-five minutes later, his light revealed a dirt wall dead ahead. He stopped as his spirits sank. Now what? He approached slowly and discovered that this wall was different than the one he had encountered yesterday. Rather than a straight wall of solid rock, this one looked like a cave-in, like rock and dirt and rubble had fallen from above. He inched closer, not sure how stable the dirt was.

Shining his light at the top, he strained to see. The mound towered above Tommy, reaching all the way to the ten foot ceiling. Was there a space between the dirt and the top of the tunnel? He couldn't be sure. Should he climb up and check? He didn't need it caving in more. He groaned. What should he do?

There were the other two off-shoot tunnels. But he had no idea how far or where those would lead. He stood for several moments, undecided. Remembering the map of the refuge, he pulled it carefully out of his jacket pocket and consulted it. To do so he had to grip the flashlight in the crook of his left arm and hold the map in his right. If they had correctly determined the position of their cavern, then one tunnel was fairly easy to eliminate. The other held possibilities.

But it was already seven-thirty in the morning and he had been gone almost ninety minutes. He should be heading back to Hunter, but then he'd only have to cover all this ground again, which seemed like a waste of time. Tommy decided to return to the two side tunnels and check out the more promising one, just for a few minutes.

The trip back to the fork seemed to take forever. Finally arriving at the spot, Tommy made an arrow on his drawing to show his direction down this side tunnel. It looked just like the others and it might lead somewhere, or not. He knew his flashlight wasn't going to last forever, yet on he trudged. It seemed endless with no way of telling if it would lead anywhere.

What an exercise in futility this seemed. He didn't have much patience for this sort of thing. If there was a way to improvise in a situation, he was happy. If it was drudgery, he lost interest fast. Still, Hunter and Spot were depending on him so he had to consider more than just himself. Another fifty minutes later, he stopped. The tunnel seemed endless.

But, how could he go back without any real progress? How could he tell Hunter he didn't know anything yet? With a heavy step, he headed back to the main tunnel and then to the cavern, arriving there about eleven-thirty.

He didn't even want to look at Hunter when he got there. What could he say? He plopped down dejectedly on the mound, tears welling up in his eyes. Why should he hide it? He could tell Hunter had been crying, too. Tommy shrugged. Hunter turned away and sobbed into his jacket sleeve.

Both boys cried for a few minutes, then Hunter sniffed, wiped his nose on his jacket and said, "Nothing, huh?"

Sniffling, Tommy said, "Nothing definite at least. The main tunnel had a cave-in. There were two side tunnels, at a sort of interchange. Looking at the refuge map, I figured one just went deeper into the mountain, so I tried the other one for almost an hour. It just kept going on and on. Who knows when or where it will end?"

"And the cave-in was impossible?" Hunter asked.

"It almost looked like there was a gap at the top, between the mound and the ceiling, but I couldn't be sure. I was afraid to climb up there, for fear of causing it to cave in more."

"Yeah, I see your point. Yet, this rock slide we're on here is stable. Maybe that one is, too."

"Maybe."

"So, it sounds like we have two main choices: try to go over the cave-in, or explore further down the side tunnel."

"Right." Tommy was impressed. Hunter wasn't giving up. In fact, Hunter's determination bolstered his own resolve.

"Right," Tommy said again, this time with more energy. "So, which should we do?"

"Well," Hunter said, "it seems to me, that the main tunnel would be more likely than a side tunnel, right? I mean, thinking of it from the other direction – they dig into the rock for the ore. At some point they make some side tunnels looking for ore. But, the original tunnel is the one that came from the outside."

"I'm impressed," Tommy said. "Your logic is great. See? It's a good thing you're in this with me, because I probably would have gone down the other tunnel."

"Really?" Hunter said with a grin.

"Really," Tommy said. "Okay, the main tunnel it is. Guess I'd better take some digging equipment this time."

"Yeah, take the other shovel and a pickaxe and the work gloves. If you, uh, if you have any trouble, use the whistle like we discussed. Okay?"

"Okay!" Tommy said, giving Hunter a high-five. Grabbing a stick of jerky he said, "Be back as soon as I can."

"I'll get everything ready here."

Tommy started off with renewed hope.

Hunter shouted after him, "Tommy – be careful."

"I will," he called over his shoulder.

Chapter Sixteen – Digging

E ven though Tommy was walking quickly, it felt like forever before he reached the broken tie and then the branch in the tunnel. Despite the cold and dampness of the passageway he was sweating.

Another forty-five minutes to the cave-in.

At last, there it was. He stopped as a chill ran down his spine. This was it – their only real hope.

Laying down the shovel and pick, he shone the light over the mound, tentatively testing a few different spots with his foot. Loose dirt gave way, but otherwise it seemed stable.

Drat his stupid injured hand. Until he picked up the shovel it hadn't been too bad today. Now, it was throbbing again. Climbing with the flashlight in the crook of his elbow was difficult and he had only one hand with which to grasp the dirt. He was more or less on his knees and good hand as he crawled up the steep rocky slope.

When he was about half way up the mound, his right foot slipped and he sprawled flat out on the rubble, the flashlight and his injured hand under him.

He lay still for a minute waiting for the jolt of pain to subside. Then, gritting his teeth, he rolled over to his left side and gingerly pulled the flashlight away from his elbow and ribs. What were a few more bruises if it got them out of there?

With a deep breath, he stuck the flashlight back in the crook of his arm and continued up the mound. Oh, please, he prayed, don't slip again.

He was almost at the top. Panting, he stopped to catch his breath, wiping the sweat from his forehead. When he thought of his mother he had to grin – she'd have a fit at how dirty his clothes were.

About eighteen inches from the top, Tommy paused. His head was going to connect with the ceiling soon and it made him feel claustrophobic.

Fighting back a shiver, he dug a slight groove with his foot, to brace himself. Placing his foot securely there, he stretched full length. With the flashlight in his right hand he shone it at the crest of the mound.

Yes! There had to be an opening there. He was sure some of the light went through. Holding the flashlight in his mouth, he reached up with his right hand. There was the top of the mound – and a space big enough for his fingers.

Hooray! Thank God! That would mean that they should be able to dig over the mound and that the passageway would continue beyond. It just might lead to the outside.

Of course, whatever caused the original cave-in might happen again. Was the ceiling unstable? Were the support beams weak or broken? If he dug through, would it just cave in more in top of him? At this point, it seemed he had to take that chance. He'd come this far, and it was the only real option left.

Gritting his teeth, he tentatively scraped a bit of the dirt away, then a little more. The dirt felt more like rock. Some of it was rock. Yet, this was their best alternative so he might as well give it a good try. Turning onto his back, he slid down the mound to the bottom, where he collected the pick. Now he had to go back up. This time he carefully carved a few footholds to help him climb.

Back near the top of the mound, he held the light in the crook of his arm again and started chipping away at the dirt above him. Progress was slow, but he didn't want to go too quickly and cause more problems.

There was a heavy rock in the way. Even though he chopped at it with the pick, it wouldn't move. As he was scraping away the dirt around it, all at once the rock dislodged and tumbled down the mound. Down came a shower of dirt and rubble, one of the larger rocks grazing him in the forehead.

Choking on the dust Tommy brushed his forehead with the back of his arm. It felt like blood, but it didn't seem too bad. He dabbed it with the sleeve of his T-shirt.

As the dust cleared, he shone the light at the top. Now there was a sizeable gap. Maybe this was going to work after all. On he chopped and scraped. His right arm was tired from digging and he wasn't exactly the in most comfortable of positions. He could feel blisters on his hand, squishing as he worked.

Turning off the flashlight he lay back against the mound. He needed a rest.

Wait a minute! He could see light! Was he imagining things? How could there be light?

Tommy scrambled to the top, cranking his head to the side to see through the gap. Light! Daylight! It must be the outside! Yay, hooray, hallelujah!

He laughed and whooped. He couldn't wait to tell Hunter. But first he should try to make more progress. Then, he and Hunter and Spot could come back and get out!

With renewed energy he scraped and dug at the wall in front of him. Chop, pull, scrape, pull. Sweat mixed with blood was trickling down his forehead. He wiped at it with his sleeve. Chop, pull, scrape, pull.

Drat. There was another big rock in the way. He chopped at the dirt around it. It moved a little. He grunted. It moved a little more. He strained at it with a heave and the boulder came free, sending Tommy flying backwards down the mound. Dirt and rocks and rubble came down all around him.

He shrieked, covering his face with his hands.

Dirt seemed to fall for an eternity. He lay still, afraid to move, afraid he couldn't move. Was he buried?

Spluttering dust and mud out of his mouth, he gasped for air. The flashlight. Where was it? Had he lost it again? The cavern was dark. Had the dirt slide covered the opening? He couldn't bear that thought.

With effort he lifted his right hand. He could get it free, so he wasn't totally buried. He moved his legs. Rubble fell away. That was good. He wiped his forehead with the back of his good hand. His left hand was throbbing, but seemed none the worse for the wear. He had to find the flashlight.

He felt all around, to the side, above his head, to the other side. He groaned. No flashlight.

Don't panic, he told himself. Just widen the search systematically. It had to be here. It had been in his left arm, but he had probably flailed as he fell, so it could have landed some distance away. Ah, yes, the lighter.

He got out the butane lighter. Thankfully, it flickered and then stayed lit. Surveying the rubble around him, Tommy thought he spotted part of the flashlight down the hill and to his left. Oh, no. It couldn't be broken again. Well, he had fixed it once, maybe he could again.

On his belly, he crawled down to the flashlight and dug it out of the rubble. It was intact. That was a piece of luck. Someone must be looking out for them. Now, did it work?

Trying the switch, he found it worked, intermittently. Maybe that would be enough for now. First, he'd dig more, and then work on it when he got back to the cavern.

Back to the top he crawled. Where had he been digging? It was all covered again and he wanted to cry. Here we go again, he thought. He found what looked like his earlier spot and scraped gingerly. He really didn't want more debris coming down on top of him.

As he shone the light on the ceiling, he could see that one of the crossbeams was broken. It was snapped nearly in two, buckled under the weight of the earth above it. A chill ran down his spine. They'd better get out of there quickly, before it collapsed even more.

He decided he'd leave as many of the bigger rocks in place as he could and just remove the loose dirt around them. The rubble from latest cave-in came loose easily, which was a good thing because his resolve was fading fast.

The opening wasn't big enough yet, not for his body. Just a little more, and gently. He needed to make the hole big enough for Hunter and him and their supplies. And of course for Spot's crate. They would need it to keep Spot in once they got out.

Glancing at his watch, he realized he'd been gone almost three hours. It was fifteen hundred hours, three o'clock Tuesday afternoon. Hunter would be expecting him anytime, but he was so close to getting through. He decided to work on, so that when he did go back to Hunter, they might be able to pack up and leave. This thought spurred him on and he dug with renewed vigor.

When a new clump of dirt fell, Tommy froze, waiting for the onslaught. It never came. With relief, he brushed the back of his forehead and continued digging. He was tired, but he had to keep going.

A large boulder filled the left side of the opening, but he decided to work around it and let it act as support for the ceiling. That meant he had to remove the dirt at the bottom of the u-shaped opening, which had been there for a long time and didn't move easily.

Was the hole big enough? Inching his way up the mound he stuck his head through the opening. His head fit, but it wasn't quite wide enough for his shoulders yet.

Before he withdrew his head, he dared a look down the tunnel. He could see the opening to the outside world! About a hundred yards down the passage was the mouth of the tunnel. He could see blue sky!

Pulling his head back in he dug frantically. He was so close. He was exhausted but he didn't feel it anymore. All he felt was an urgency to make the opening large enough, and then to go back for Hunter and Spot. He had no more sense of time – he only knew he had to finish this hole.

Tommy crawled to the top again and verified that he could fit through the hole, hoping they'd be able to get Spot's crate through, too, though he couldn't be sure. It would have to do for now. Sliding back down to the tunnel floor, he left the shovel and pickaxe so he could carry more on his return and barely resisted the urge to run back to the cavern.

Chapter Seventeen - A Way Out?

Tommy couldn't contain himself as he approached the cavern. He ran in jumping and shouting.

"I got through! I got through! I've seen daylight and it's wonderful!"

"All right!" Hunter shouted and gave Tommy a high-five. The boys lay on the mound cheering and laughing.

"Come on," said Hunter. "Let's get out of here! I can't wait to leave this dungeon behind!"

"Yeah!" Tommy said. "Why don't we make a sled to drag all the stuff on?"

Hunter agreed, so the boys picked one of the biggest planks to drag their supplies on. They found one that had a few nails in it and wrapped their cord around the nails to make some reins.

After helping Hunter put on Tommy's backpack, they strapped Spot's crate onto the plank, covering the crate with a piece of the plywood and taping it on with duct tape. The rest of their gear they piled in front of the crate and covered it with their jackets. It was seventeen hundred hours, or five p.m. when they began their journey to the outside world.

The trip was not without problems. It was slow-going for Hunter, hobbling with the shovel as a crutch and he had to stop numerous times to rest. Tommy had difficulties as well because the cord from the reins dug into his waist and items kept slipping and shifting on their makeshift sled. To add to the troubles, the feline passenger, not at all happy with the lurching and jolting, did not go quietly.

It took them two hours to get to the cave-in. Once there, they set down their loads and Tommy helped Hunter claw his way up the pile of rubble to the opening.

"I can't believe it!" Hunter cried. "Daylight. The outside world!"

Tommy could hardly believe it either. He had thought they might never see it again. He beamed at Hunter, pumped his fist, and shouted, "Go for it!"

Hunter squeezed through the opening and slid down the rubble on his belly on the other side, landing with a thud and a yelp on the tunnel floor.

"What happened?" called Tommy.

"It's nothing," Hunter said with a laugh. "I

just scraped my nose on the floor." Both boys chuckled.

Tommy tore at the sled with fervor. He had to take everything apart to get it through the hole. Peering through the opening he began to push stuff through to Hunter.

Hunter rolled over and sat up as the supplies began to bump him. Catching them as they slid down, he piled them beside him. Next came the plank with nails and cord.

"Oh, no," Tommy groaned.

"What?" said Hunter.

"Spot's crate won't fit." He grunted, trying to force it. The hole was the wrong shape. "Well, let's just take him without the crate," Hunter suggested.

"But we need something to keep him in. He's not strong enough yet to release."

"I know that, but maybe we can find or make something else. You're good at making things, you know."

"Yeah, but this crate is so perfect. Maybe if I just dig a little bit more."

"Tommy," Hunter whined. "We're so close, how can you wait?"

"Tell you what. You go on ahead. Leave all the stuff. I'll bring it in a minute."

Hunter looked longingly at the tunnel entrance. "I'm not going without you," he insisted.

"Are you sure?" asked Tommy.

"Of course."

"Gee, Hunter, thanks. This will just take a second." With the pick he chopped and pushed soil away from the hole until there was enough room. Hunter crawled up to help from the other side.

With Tommy pushing and Hunter tugging, they forced Spot's crate through the opening, but not without a chorus of protesting yowls from the feline. At last everything was on the other side, except for Tommy and the pick and shovel. As Tommy slid down to retrieve the shovel he heard dirt falling behind him.

"Tommy!" Hunter screamed.

Tommy barely had time to grab the pick again and throw himself at the opening. Dirt was falling fast. He shoved the pick through and heaved as hard as he could with both arms. Hunter grabbed his shirt and tugged.

"Get back, Hunter!" Tommy shouted. "Save yourself and Spot. Get away!"

"No, I'm not leaving you!" Hunter cried, tugging with all his strength.

But Tommy was stuck. His ankles were pinned by the dirt and rubble which had caved yet another time.

"Oh, no," Hunter whined. "What are we going to do, Tommy? We can't leave you here."

Tommy could see that Hunter was fighting back tears. He managed a calm voice and said, "What we're going to do is, you are going to get yourself and Spot and our supplies out of here. By the time everything is outside, maybe I'll be loose.

I'll use the pick to free myself while you're doing the rest. Deal?"

Hunter bit back a sob. "Okay. I'll do it, but you're not giving up, you hear? I'll be right back for you. Be really careful as you dig."

"I will." He watched as Hunter hobbled toward the outside, trying to drag Spot in his crate on the plank.

Tommy surveyed his predicament. Once he got his legs free, well, okay, if he got his legs free, he would have to run to get out of the tunnel. No telling how much more might collapse. He'd better wait until Hunter had all of the supplies outside.

He could see Hunter pull Spot outside and set the baby bobcat off to the side of the tunnel entrance. Then, Hunter returned to collect more of their stuff. He set it on the plank and limped his way back toward the entrance, stopping once to replace items that had slipped off.

Along the wall of the tunnel, Tommy could see something silhouetted against the light. What could that be? If he had time later, he'd check it out.

When Hunter had off-loaded the last of the supplies and was headed back, Tommy began chipping at the soil pinning him. It was hard work because he couldn't get any leverage. He tried twisting this way and that to free himself, but with little success.

"Hunter," he called, "Don't come any closer. Once I'm free, I'm making a break for the outside."

"But, can you do it alone? Maybe I can help."

"Yes, but then you might not get out. Wait there. Let me see how I do."

Little by little, he loosened the soil holding him prisoner. With a grunt, he dug the pick into the mound in front of him and pulled with all his might. His arm was so tired from all the digging that he hardly had any strength, but his body budged slightly. Straining, he pulled more and moved a few more inches.

With huge effort he tucked his knees and jerked his feet free from the dirt. He rolled down the mound and landed at the bottom, the pick in his hand clanging as it hit the hard tunnel floor. Tommy could hear dirt falling behind him. Not even waiting to catch his breath, he leaped to his feet and dashed toward the tunnel opening, almost tripping over a wooden pallet holding several large metal drums.

"Go, Hunter! Run!" he yelled as he neared the entrance. He could see Hunter silhouetted against the light just ahead of him. They both reached the outside as a cloud of dust belched from the tunnel.

"Wow, that was close," Hunter panted.

"No lie," said Tommy with a shudder. He plopped down on the ground beside the tunnel opening, gasping for air. His heart was still thumping.

Hugging each other and laughing, the boys cried tears of joy. Their whoops of laughter died to giggles and they lay on the warm stone and relaxed. It was the first time they had been warm in days.

"Hunter, thanks so much. I – I – well, thanks for staying with me."

Hunter stared at Tommy. "Huh, I've never done anything like that before."

"Well, you've done it now. Thanks."

Hunter grinned shyly. "You bet."

Tommy sighed as he saw the desert floor stretched out below them. It was wonderful to be able to see farther than ten feet in front of them and to see sky and plants and open space, instead of dirt and stone walls.

He could hardly believe they had made it out. But now what? Now they had to survive above ground, in the heat and relentless sun, until they could get rescued. Was this going to be any better?

Chapter Eighteen - Beacons and Markers

At last, Tommy and Hunter and Spot were out of their dungeon and above ground. It was Tuesday evening about nineteen-thirty, or seven-thirty and daylight was fading fast.

Tommy could feel the warmth from the soil and stones beneath him and it felt wonderful. Drinking in his beloved desert surroundings he sighed contentedly.

He found himself on a rocky mountainside. Behind him was the tunnel opening looming like a gaping black mouth. The mountain, made of dark volcanic rock, rose almost straight up behind him. Even though there was little soil and almost no vegetation, here and there a brave, scraggly creosote bush clung to the stark mountainside.

Below him the slope was more gradual as it

descended to the valley floor. The black volcanic rock was covered with a thin layer of topsoil, which became deeper as it reached the valley floor, yielding increasing numbers of creosote, tall saguaro, teddy bear cholla, and other varieties of cactus. Even some little leaf palo verde trees were still green with fresh growth from the late spring rains.

The sky had never looked so beautiful to Tommy before. Both boys watched as the sun dropped behind the mountain range behind them and the brilliant sunset faded from orange to red-orange to purple and then a dusky blue.

Hunter spoke. "So, now what? We've been so focused on getting out of the mine, now what happens?"

"Yeah, I guess we'd better build a fire for the night. It's going to get pretty cold now that the sun is going down."

The two boys cleared a spot for a fire ring on a level spot about twenty yards from the tunnel opening. While Tommy collected the stones Hunter placed them in a circle. Tommy gathered sticks and dead branches from the palo verde trees and creosote bushes and they built a small fire.

"Too bad we don't have something to cook," Hunter commented, "but the fire feels great, anyway."

"Sure does," Tommy agreed, feeling on top of the world.

They celebrated their emergence from the cave by finishing their trail mix and the rest of their

Gatorade water, and several sticks of jerky. There was still about half a gallon of untreated water in the thermos, but Tommy knew that wouldn't last more than one day.

Snuggled near the fire, the boys slept off and on through the night. Whenever one awoke, he tossed more sticks on the fire to keep it going.

Wednesday morning dawned bright and clear. Tommy inhaled the fresh air deeply, stretched and sat up. Hunter was still sleeping. Reaching inside his backpack Tommy pulled out one of the two clear plastic bags and made his way to a large creosote bush not far away.

Nursing his sore left hand, he carefully pulled several of the branches together and tied them loosely with some thread from his Swiss Army knife sewing kit. Then he placed the plastic bag loosely around the branches and drew the opening together. Using more string he tied the opening shut. He had to be very careful not to puncture the bag or the makeshift transpiration still would be lost. Finally, he gently pulled a corner of the bag down so that the moisture would run into the pocket.

He almost jumped when he heard a voice behind him. "What are you doing?" Hunter asked, rubbing his eyes as he sat up.

"Making water," Tommy replied simply.

"Wow, too cool," said Hunter as he joined Tommy at the bush. "The moisture condenses inside the bag, making water. Is that one of the tricks Pete was going to teach us on this trip?"

"Probably. Gosh, I wonder how everyone else is doing."

"They're probably worried sick about us. Bet they don't even think we're alive."

"It's amazing that we are."

"Yeah," Hunter agreed quietly. "So, that's water. Now, where's the food?"

"We're going to have to make that, too. We're lucky spring was late this year. There might be some fruit on some of the cacti. Remember the saguaro we saw blooming? Those flowers turn into fruit that is edible. Many of the cacti have edible fruit."

"Right. Guess we'll look for some?"

"Okay, why don't you do these close ones? I'll check those over there.

"Deal," said Hunter.

"Remember the spines are really sharp. And watch out for snakes," Tommy called over his shoulder as he left.

"Snakes? Where will the snakes be?"

"In crevices and under rocks. Just stay out in the open and you should be okay. We don't have very long. The sun will be getting really hot soon."

"Right," Hunter muttered as he hobbled on his crutch toward a nearby saguaro.

A short while later both boys met back at the campfire. In his one free arm, Hunter carried a dozen green pods.

"I found these under that saguaro. Are they what you meant?" He asked.

"Yes, those should be them. I think if we break them open, there will be fruit inside."

"You're sure they're not poisonous?"

"No, I mean, yes, I'm sure they're not poisonous. If they came from the saguaro, they're safe to eat. They look like the ones Mr. Steinman brought to science class last year. Let's try them."

Tommy peeled one open with his knife. Inside was the bright red juicy pulp he had hoped for.

"Yes! Way to go, Hunter. Here, try some."

"Well, I don't know. You go ahead."

Tommy grinned and sucked the juicy fruit out of the pod. He flinched as the tart, sweet mixture reached his tongue.

"Boy," he said, "it sure is good to taste something besides water and carrots. Come on, I'm sure it's okay." He offered Hunter another pod.

Cautiously the other boy took one and peeled it open. He gave Tommy an uncertain look before slowly poking his tongue at the fruit. It must have seemed okay because he licked again and then slurped the fruit out of the shell.

Both boys laughed as Hunter shuddered from the tart taste. Before long they had consumed a dozen saguaro fruit pods and chased them down with water.

Even Spot got into the act. Tommy peeled open a pod and pried the pulp out, laying it on a slat of the kitten's cage. Spot sniffed tentatively, and then licked it up in one gulp. Tommy chuckled. The boys took turns sharing saguaro fruit with their feline companion.

Tommy knew that if they wanted to be found they had to have some way to help the search parties locate them, so their next task was to make some sort of marker or beacon for the searchers to spot.

He picked a site farther down on the valley floor where he could build a marker. It needed to be away from bushes as much as possible, so it would stand out. He hiked down to the intended spot and selected a number of large boulders, as dark in coloration as he could find, so they would stand out against the desert sand.

Clearing the area of brush and other large rocks, he shoved the darker boulders into a straight line. To form an arrow tip he placed more boulders at the top, pointing to their campsite farther up the hill.

As he headed back to the campsite, Tommy noticed several circling vultures on the other side of the mouth of the tunnel. He'd have to check that out later. By the time he returned it was already almost ten a.m. and he was sweating profusely.

"I'd better rest a minute," he panted as he plopped down.

"Here, I made some more Gatorade water," Hunter said. "And maybe we should go sit in the shade of the tunnel opening. It's getting awfully hot out here, and I'm not even doing much."

Tommy pulled the thermometer out of his back pack. "Gosh, it's already 95 degrees!"

After Tommy helped Hunter up the hill to the mouth of the tunnel, where the temperature was easily fifteen degrees cooler, he made a trip back to collect Spot.

"What else can we do to get rescued?" asked Hunter.

"We need to keep the fire going, though it's not very big, so it will be hard to see from the air. We could tie my extra bandana onto a high branch of one of the palo verde trees. They might be able to notice that, if they're using binoculars. If we spot any kind of plane overhead we can signal with my mirror. There's not much left of it, but I think it will be enough to signal with."

"Okay. We should have everything ready since we never know when a plane will pass overhead."

"Good idea. As soon as we cool down a bit, I can tie my orange bandana on that palo verde over there, and then try practicing with my mirror. You can make another transpiration still."

"Meanwhile, I sure would like something solid to eat," Hunter said. "Any suggestions?"

"Not unless we find a snake or a mouse or some other animal."

"I hear rabbit's not too bad. Tastes like chicken."

"I don't know if I could eat a rabbit," Tommy said.

"I'm hungry enough to eat just about anything."

"Well, you know, part of my motto as a

veterinarian is to save animal life, not take it. The Latin saying, *"Primum non nocere –* means "First, do no harm." Now, a snake, maybe I could manage that, but only if it was threatening us."

"Well, I don't particularly want to meet a snake!" Hunter protested.

"No, me either," admitted Tommy. "But I guess when it comes right down to it, we may not have much choice. Depending on how long it takes them to find us, we may just have to eat what we can get."

After a rest in the mouth of the tunnel, the boys set about their separate chores, leaving Spot in his crate in the shade.

Tommy explained to Hunter how to make a second still on a nearby creosote. While Hunter made the still and soaked off the remaining water in the thermos into their water bottles, Tommy took his orange bandana and headed for the palo verde tree. After several attempts, the signal flag waved in a slight breeze on a top branch of the tree.

Returning to the campsite, Tommy got out the remainder of his broken mirror, a jagged piece about two and a half inches square, and practiced signaling with it. After cutting himself, he decided to put some duct tape over the broken edge. He selected a rock a short distance away and tried hitting it with the beam of light reflected from his mirror. With some practice he was able to fairly accurately place the beam where he wanted it.

He practiced flashing the universal SOS signal – dot, dot, dot, dash, dash, dash, dot, dot, dot.

Clumsy at first, he soon was feeling more comfortable with it. Now all they needed was a passing aircraft that could see the signal.

Chapter Nineteen – Snake!

Once again, feeling the intense heat, the boys headed for the shade of the mine tunnel.

Tommy said, "Let's take my binoculars. At least we can look at things while we wait."

"Good idea," Hunter agreed.

Arriving at the tunnel entrance, Tommy stooped to look at Spot. "Hey, little one, would you like out of your crate for a while? How would it be if we let you roam around on your leash? But, don't go far." He set a heavy rock on the loose end of the kitten's leash.

The boys took their positions in the mouth of the tunnel and Tommy trained the binoculars on the valley floor.

"Hey," he said. "I can see the arrow I made to point to our campsite."

"Cool," said Hunter. "Now let's just hope someone else sees it."

"No lie," Tommy agreed.

"Any airplanes?" Hunter asked.

"No, afraid not."

Both boys were silent as they stared out at the desert landscape before them. Spot mewed as he nudged Tommy's elbow.

"You're hungry, too, aren't you, little one?" Tommy said. "Your mama should be taking care of you and teaching you how to hunt for food. I know she'd be here for you if she could, so something bad must have happened to her."

Tommy picked up the kitten and inspected him. "You are so cute," he murmured, gently fingering the soft tan and brown and white fur. Spot's golden green eyes gazed back at Tommy. They showed no fear.

"He trusts you," said Hunter.

"Yes, and that's good and bad." To Spot, Tommy said, "I'd love to hold you all the time, Spot, but that's not a good idea. I want you to be releasable back here on the refuge when you're stronger, and if you get too tame, that won't happen. It may be too late already, but I hope not."

"I love his markings," Hunter said. "Look, those dark streaks under his chin almost form a necklace. He's beautiful."

"Yes, he is. Hey, maybe we should have

called him 'Smiley'. See how the shape of his muzzle almost forms a smile?"

"Yeah," Hunter replied, grinning, "but I like 'Spot' better. How old do you think he is?"

"It's hard to tell because he's so skinny. We don't know how long he's been undernourished, or how long his mother's been gone, but I'd guess he's about two-and-a-half or three months old. He seems younger than the one we worked on at the clinic last week."

"When I learned I'd be coming on this expedition," Hunter said, "I did some research on the Internet. Mother bobcats usually have litters of two to four kittens in the spring and the kittens stay with their mothers for almost a year, so Spot should have another nine months of training from his mom."

"Yes, poor little guy. I wonder how he got caught in the mine shaft. If the shaft was covered and gave way under you, then he must have fallen in after you did. But he's so skinny and dehydrated, I'd bet he's been on his own for a while."

"So, where's his mom?"

"That's the mystery," Tommy said.

Gazing through the binoculars again, Tommy said, "Wait, I can see something coming – in the air – coming this way. It's a hawk and it's got something in its talons!"

"Oh," Hunter groaned. "I thought you saw an airplane."

"No, sorry, but this hawk is gorgeous. And

he's getting closer. You look." He handed the binoculars to Hunter.

"Wow," said Hunter, "he's coming right toward us. What's that he's carrying? Yikes, it's a snake!"

"Hunter, look!" Tommy pointed. "Another hawk. He's a lot bigger. They're so close now I don't even need the binoculars."

"They're fighting!" Hunter exclaimed.

The boys watched in awe as the two birds of prey swooped and dove and screeched, performing a mid-air tug-of-war over the quarry.

Suddenly, the snake fell from the grasp of the smaller hawk and it dove to recapture it, but was knocked off course by the aggressor. For several more seconds the hawks were locked in battle, until the smaller bird fled back in the direction from which it had come. The majestic larger hawk circled a few times and flew away.

"Gosh, that was really something," Hunter said. "I guess the little guy lost his supper."

"Yes, I wonder why the big one didn't go after it."

"I wish he had. Do you think the snake is still alive?" asked Hunter with a shiver.

"I don't know. After a fall from that height, it very well might be dead."

"Let's hope so, but did you see where it fell?" Hunter said. "It landed right by our camp."

"Near it, maybe," Tommy said. "If it is alive, it won't bother us. It will hide under rocks to stay cool."

"Well, maybe." Hunter sounded doubtful. "But I don't think I want to sleep there anymore."

"It'll be okay, Hunter," Tommy reassured. But he had to admit, it gave him the creeps, too. Neither one of them could afford to get bitten by a rattlesnake.

Chapter Twenty – Snake Steak

As the heat began to wane, Tommy said, "Time to go back to the campsite, I guess."

"I'm not going," said Hunter. "With that snake there, I'm not going anywhere near it."

Exasperated, Tommy stared at Hunter. Now what? He didn't like the idea of leaving Hunter in the cave alone over night, even if it was only a few yards from their camp. It was just better if they stayed together.

"I'll tell you what," Tommy offered. "I'll go investigate the area. If I don't find the snake will you come?"

The other boy hesitated. "I don't know."

"Look, I'll clear the area all around the camp. Like I said, snakes hide under rocks to stay cool. If there aren't any rocks around the camp, we should be safe. Okay?"

"Why can't we just stay here?"

"Being near the fire is a better idea. It keeps the wildlife away. Besides, it'll be really cold here."

Hunter was silent.

Gritting his teeth in frustration, Tommy said, "I'm going to go check." With that, he stomped down the hillside, making plenty of noise just in case the snake was lurking nearby.

Beginning at the fire ring, Tommy slowly worked his way outward in a widening circle, tapping the ground with a creosote branch he had picked up on his way down. Nothing stirred. There were only three rocks large enough to hide a snake and they were each more than twenty feet from the camp. Still, he'd better check them out or he'd never get Hunter to come back.

Carefully, he approached the first boulder. Tapping it and checking all around it, he found no sign of the snake. Heading for the second rock, which was on the far side of the camp and farther down the hill, Tommy froze.

There was the snake, lying partially hidden by a creosote bush. Tommy watched breathlessly for several moments, but there was no sign of movement from the snake. Slowly, he stooped to pick up a stone and then tossed it at the reptile. It didn't move. He tossed another stone. Nothing.

He could see that it was a large western diamond back rattler, about four feet in length. The tan of the scaly skin was marked by the series of telltale darker brown diamond-shaped patterns from head to tail.

"Sorry, pal," Tommy said to the snake. "I guess you would have been killed by the hawk anyway, but I'm sorry you had to die."

Maybe now Hunter would be willing to come back to the fire. Tommy had to admit he was secretly relieved, too.

Fetching the pickaxe from the campsite, Tommy chopped off the snake's head and buried it because he knew that the fangs were lethal even if the snake was dead. Using a forked branch, he carried the decapitated snake back to the shelter of the tunnel because it was still too hot to work in the sun.

"Well, looks like we have dinner," Tommy said.

Hunter grimaced. "Eew. Maybe I'm not so hungry."

"Not very appetizing in this form," Tommy agreed, "but it'll be okay once it's cooked."

"Wow, it's really big. Where did you find it?"

"It was about twenty feet from the fire ring, pretty much hidden under a creosote. I guess that's why the bigger hawk didn't see it."

"Did you kill it?"

"No, thankfully it was already dead, probably from the fall. I don't know if I could have killed it."

"I'm sorry I was such a chicken, Tommy."

"It's okay, I understand. It creeps me out,

too. I checked all around the camp fire and it's all clear. I really think it will be safe to go back."

"Okay. You're probably right."

As the sun began to set, the boys took Spot and returned to their campsite. Hunter stoked the fire while Tommy started preparing the snake.

He had never skinned and gutted a snake before, but he thought he could figure out how to do it. He had seen enough on the farm. While he worked on the snake, he put Spot back in his cage. Using some of the murky water from the bottom of the thermos, he proceeded to slice the snake up the belly and pull out the innards.

It took him some time to skin the snake because he was limited with his damaged hand. Weighting the neck of the snake down with a rock from the fire ring, Tommy nearly succeeded in pulling off the skin in one complete strip. He chopped off the rattle and set it aside for Hunter, who had busied himself with checking one of the water stills.

"Hey, Tommy, look. There's a lot of water in here. This thing's pretty cool."

"It's all right, huh? Don't puncture it when you untie it, and then pour the water into the bottles, okay?"

"Will do."

By the time Hunter was finished emptying the water still, Tommy had dinner ready. He had cut the snake into five sections and skewered them on cleaned branches from a nearby palo verde tree and then roasted them over the fire. The juice from the snake dripping into the fire caused it to flare brightly.

"Wow, that smells great," Hunter said. Spot was mewing loudly. It smelled good to him, too.

"It's ready. Come and get it."

Tommy handed Hunter the rattle from the snake's tail. It had ten joints.

"You can show this as your trophy when we get back."

"Yeah."

Tommy could tell from the tone of Hunter's voice that he questioned that possibility.

"Come on, let's eat," Tommy urged. With a flourish and in his best British butler accent he announced, "Dinner is served. Our main course this evening will be snake steak."

"With crystal water à la creosote still," added Hunter.

The boys laughed and enjoyed their meal as they had few others.

Tommy crawled over to Spot's crate with a piece of meat. Barely had he laid it on the slat, before the kitten had snatched it up. He was glad they had something to feed Spot. This baby was dependent on them.

As they sat around the fire, they began to hear night noises coming from the desert.

"Oww, ooww, ooowww!" came the mournful cry of a coyote. Quickly came a reply. It was as though they were talking to each other.

"I wish I could see them," Tommy whispered. "They're gorgeous. They're really not aggressive, so I'm sure they won't attack us. In fact, they often like humans. Here on the refuge, they may be pretty used to people."

"Still, they sound spooky." Hunter shivered. "Spot doesn't seem to like them, either. We better make sure we have enough wood for the fire tonight."

"Good idea. Why don't I dump it here and you can break it up."

"Deal."

Later, wood collected and chopped, the boys bedded down for the night. They stretched out head to head around their fire ring. Wood was within reach to stoke the fire if either woke up. They lay there talking quietly as night deepened and the fire burned lower.

"Things didn't exactly go the way Ranger Peterson planned, did they?" said Hunter.

"That's for sure," Tommy agreed. "I could see pretty quickly that Matt and Andy were going to be jerks, but it never occurred to me they would do something as mean as they did."

"Well, I was totally stupid falling for it, but you know, being new and all – I guess I just wanted to fit in. Kind of backfired for all of us, huh?"

"That's an understatement!"

"Do you think we're going to get out of this, Tommy?"

"Yes, I do. I think we've done really well getting this far, and we can take care of ourselves for some time yet, but we need to do all we can to help them find us."

"Do you think they're still looking?"

"Sure. I know they won't give up. It's only been four days so far. We ought to be able to attract search planes somehow. The rock marker and the mirror signal should help. If we could get the fire going really strongly and get a lot of smoke, that would help, too."

"Tomorrow let's look for more wood," Hunter said through a yawn.

"Shh! Hunter, look! Slowly, see it over there? You can see the golden eyes. It's a coyote. He's watching us." Tommy was grinning so wide his sunburned face hurt.

"Whoa, he's really close," Hunter whispered.

"He won't hurt us, I'm sure. He probably smells the roasted snake, but being so close he makes Spot nervous." The little feline cowered in a corner of his crate.

Cautiously, Tommy reached for a leftover scrap of the snake meat lying at the edge of the fire. He lifted it slowly, then tossed it off to the side. The coyote followed it with his eyes, then retreated. A moment later they could hear it eating the snake meat. Tommy chuckled.

"Cool," Hunter agreed.

"When we get back, I'll show you the clinic. It's really neat."

"I'll bet it is."

Tommy slept better that night than he had on the whole trip. He felt relaxed and content being so near the wildlife he loved. Still, he wondered how long it would take before they were rescued. Would they really be able to make their resources last?

Chapter Twenty-one – A Grizzly Discovery

Thursday morning dawned bright and clear. Tommy awoke to the melodies of a western mockingbird. Turning his head carefully so he wouldn't disturb the songster he spotted the bird perched on top of the same palo verde that bore his orange bandana. He smiled as it reminded him of the bird that often perched in the tamarisk tree where he had his fort.

Hunter woke soon after Tommy, and the boys set about clearing the fire and getting ready for another day. Things began much the same as they had the day before. When the heat became too much, the boys took Spot on his leash and retreated to the shelter of the tunnel opening with the binoculars. "Hey, where's the map of the refuge?" Tommy asked, peering intently into the binoculars.

Hunter's head snapped to look at Tommy. "You have it, don't you?"

"Oh, yeah, I guess I do." Tommy stretched out and reached in his shorts' pocket. The map was tattered, and tore even more when he extracted it. With great care, he spread it out on the tunnel floor in front of them.

"I estimate we're about here," he said, pointing to a place on the map.

"I think so, too," said Hunter.

If their guess was correct, there was a water hole not far from them.

"Maybe I could check out the water hole," Tommy said.

"I don't know, Tommy," Hunter said. "We don't know how far away it is. Besides, we're not one-hundred-percent sure of our location. I think it's too risky."

"But we can't just sit here forever," Tommy said, handing the binoculars to Hunter. Tommy's urge to keep busy was eating at him. He hated to just sit and wait.

"You know our best bet for being found is to stay in the same place. The more we move around, the harder it is for anyone to find us."

"I know. I just can't stand sitting around. I've got to have something to do." He stood up and paced about in the tunnel entrance. Suddenly, a flash of panic ran through his body. "Where's Spot?" he exclaimed.

"What?" cried Hunter. "He was right here!"

"Oh, my gosh," cried Tommy. "Where did he go?"

Grabbing his flashlight, Tommy dashed into the tunnel. "Spot! Spot! Here boy," he called.

Frantically, he searched along the passage way. Coming to the barrels off to the side, he shone the light behind the containers and around the pallets on which they rested. No Spot, but a yellow skull and cross bones poison indicator was plastered on each barrel.

"Spot!" he called, racing toward the cave-in. There was no sign of the little feline. He couldn't have gone farther, so that meant he had to be outside the tunnel.

Dashing back to the cave entrance, Tommy reported, "He's not in there – he must be outside." Leaving his flashlight he snatched up the binoculars and panned as full-circle as he could see. Up the hill behind them, over toward their camp, down the mountainside to the valley floor. Nothing.

"I have to go look for him," Tommy said. "I think he's too young and weak to survive on his own."

Hunter groaned. "Tommy, please be careful. With me all laid up, you really need to take care of yourself. If anything happens to you, we're sunk."

"Okay, I promise I'll be careful. Pray I find him."

Where could Spot have gone? Tommy wondered. He could be almost anywhere. Off to his right, Tommy spotted the vultures again. It had to be something dead or dying. Maybe Spot would head for other creatures. Tommy decided to start looking there.

Hunter called something after him, but Tommy couldn't hear it over the crunching of his own boots on the dirt.

He was zig-zagging, cutting sideways across the hill and up. It was hot and the way was steep with no path and in no time at all he was sweating profusely. His injured left hand hindered any steep climbing, so he had to take the longer way around a large outcropping of rocks.

As he paused to rest, he heard a sound. Mewing. Spot!

Tommy scrambled on in the direction of the sound.

A few minutes later, he rounded the bottom edge of the rocks and halted. Spot was crying and straining against his rope which was caught around a large boulder.

"Spot!" Tommy exclaimed, snatching up the wayward kitten. "I'm so glad I found you," he murmured, hugging the feline close and freeing its rope.

Then Tommy noticed. There, a few yards in front of him was a small pool of water. Beside the water lay a rotting carcass. Tommy felt his skin crawl and his stomach churn. He shuddered. What was it?

Flies swarmed around and atop it. When he picked up a pebble and tossed it, the movement stirred the flies and they retreated. It looked like more than one body, though there wasn't much left but the spotted fur. Spot's mother? His brother or sister?

Tommy stood and stared, his heart aching. There must be something wrong with the water. "It's a good thing you didn't get to that water," he told Spot, cradling the little animal tenderly.

But, what could have ruined the water hole?

With a shiver he remembered the barrels he had just seen again in the tunnel. What was in them? There must be an underground water stream that fed this hole.

This was awful. How many of the water holes were affected? Who could be leaving this stuff here and what was it? Too many questions. No answers.

Fighting down a shudder, Tommy turned and hurried back to the tunnel.

He plopped down in the shade of the tunnel opening, breathing heavily from his exertion.

"Spot!" Hunter cried with joy. "You bad little boy, scaring us like that. Where did you find him?" he asked Tommy in amazement.

"There's a small water hole over there, but the water's bad. There are a couple of carcasses beside it." He wiped his forehead with his hand. "Bobcats, I think." He wanted to cry.

"Thank heavens Spot's rope got hung up on a boulder and he couldn't get to the water," Tommy finished.

"Eew," said Hunter. "Really yucky?"

"Yeah, pretty bad. May be Spot's mother, who knows?"

"Oh," said Hunter, his face falling. "What's wrong with the water?" he asked.

"Did you see those barrels in the tunnel when he came out?"

Hunter's eyes grew wide. "Toxic waste?"

Tommy nodded. "Yes, there are poison markings all over them. Meanwhile, we have to do something to stop more animals from using that bad water hole. And you, little Spot, we have to keep a better eye on you," Tommy said, tying the free end of the rope around his own ankle.

Chapter Twenty-two – Mending the Still

For most of the rest of Thursday afternoon, the boys sat in the cave. Tommy was troubled by what he had seen and didn't feel much like talking. He had to do something to cover that water hole, so no other animals could use it and die. Finally, he explained his plan to Hunter and headed for the water hole, leaving Spot tied to Hunter's good leg.

Nearly two hours later, Tommy returned, hot and tired, but satisfied. He had taken every rock that he could move and piled it over the water and the carcasses. He just hoped it would deter any other animals.

That night the coyote returned to watch their campfire, but the boys had nothing to offer the curious canine. Tommy hoped desperately that the animal wouldn't drink from the tainted pond.

By Friday, the boys were hungry again for meat, but weren't about to go looking for a snake. They contented themselves with searching for different kinds of fruit. Tommy knew that besides the saguaro, there were several other types of cactus that also bore edible fruit.

Within relatively easy reach, there were teddy bear cholla, barrel cacti, clusters of hedgehog cacti, and even a few prickly pear farther up the mountain side. Hobbling on his crutch Hunter investigated the closer ones, while Tommy checked out the more distant ones.

Half an hour later, Tommy met Hunter at the fire ring and set down his load of fifteen bright yellow fruit he had harvested from a barrel cactus. Discovering that they needed to refill their water bottles, he chose the bag with less water in it and untied the string around the bag. As he turned with the bag, his foot slipped and the bag snagged on the bush and ripped. The water poured out – onto the ground.

"No!" Tommy yelled. "Oh, no!"

Hunter reached out to catch the bag, but by this time, it was empty. Tommy sagged to the ground.

"Oh, man. I can't believe I did that. We need that water. We need that bag!"

Hunter stared at Tommy then back at the torn bag in his own hand.

"Well," he said quietly. "We do still have

one bag. We'll just have to be really careful with it."

"I was being careful," snapped Tommy. "At least I was trying to be."

"You're always careful with things, Tommy, but with one hand, it's just – well – awkward."

Tommy knew Hunter was trying to reassure him, but he still felt awful. They needed water to survive. What if his actions were the cause of their doom? He couldn't bear that thought. He had to do something. He wanted so badly to fix the situation. He stared at Hunter and gulped.

Hunter spoke quietly. "It's okay, Tommy. We'll figure something out."

"No, it's not okay, Hunter!" Tommy shouted, his good fist clenched by his side. "I've ruined the bag and lost the water and we need it and – and -" he broke off with a sob.

"So, you're not perfect. You blow things just like any of the rest of us."

"Yeah, well, my blunder may cost us our lives! I can't deal with that."

"You forget that it was me that got us into this mess in the first place. How do you think I feel?"

"Well, but, yeah, but –"

"And you haven't condemned me. You stuck up for me. You kept giving me more chances." Hunter's voice cracked. "Tommy, you don't know how much that's meant to me. And maybe you need that sometimes, too, you know?"

Tommy looked at Hunter. "I – I don't know what to say."

"I know. It's okay."

They decided to work on the remaining water-still bag together. With Tommy's good right hand and Hunter's left hand, they managed to pour the water into their drinking bottles.

"Hey! I've got it," Hunter said. "Why can't we duct tape the bag back together and use it again? It's not so badly torn that we can't repair it, is it?"

"Great idea, Hunter."

With a few strips of duct tape, the bag was back in service. It took both of them to reattach it to the tree, but soon it was again producing water.

After taking a break in the shade of the tunnel opening, Tommy gathered fruit from some nearby hedgehog cacti. Using a stick, he knocked the purplish fruit from the spiny clumps of plant.

"Wow, those cacti look nasty," Hunter said as Tommy delivered his pickings to the campsite. "It's amazing how many different types there are. They really are kind of pretty."

"The desert isn't so bad, is it?" Tommy said.

"No, although I hope we don't have to stay out here too much longer," Hunter said with a grin.

The boys bedded down to the sounds of howling coyotes and a crackling campfire.

How much longer would they have to stay there? Tommy wondered.

Chapter Twenty-three – Visitors in the Night

Nestled by the campfire, Tommy awoke suddenly several hours later. What was that noise?

"Hunter!" he whispered. "Hunter, wake up. What's that sound?"

Both boys listened intently.

"A truck?" Hunter said.

The boys stared at each other in the faded firelight.

"They've found us!" Hunter shouted. "Someone's found us!" He was struggling to get up as he finished his sentence.

Tommy said, "Where is it? Can you tell?"

"Where's the flashlight?" asked Hunter. Both boys were groping around their campsite for the flashlight.

"Here it is," Tommy said. "I've been trying to keep it in my backpack, so we could find it easily."

"Where are they? Where's the truck?" shouted Hunter.

"The flashlight's not very strong anymore," said Tommy. He shook it and tapped it on his leg. It still wasn't working very dependably. "It sounds like it's on the other side of the mountain. We have to signal!"

"Yes, try it! Where's your whistle?"

Tommy pulled the whistle from around his neck. Hunter blew on the whistle while Tommy flashed SOS with the flashlight. Meanwhile, Spot was wailing in his cage, spooked by all the uproar.

Then there was another sound. "Shh," said Tommy. The boys listened again. "A helicopter?" Tommy said.

"Wow, they really have found us!" Hunter shouted.

Tommy and Hunter bounced up and down, flashing the light, blowing the whistle.

"Hey!" Tommy yelled, waving his arms wildly. "Hey!" But the chopper hovered over the far side of their mountain, never coming any closer to the boys.

"What are they doing?" cried Hunter. "Can't they see us over here?"

Tommy was puzzled. Maybe the people couldn't hear them over their own vehicle noise and the chopper rotor blades. He stooped and grabbed a branch, sticking it in the fire so it caught brightly.

He waved it back and forth in a wide, sweeping motion. "Hey!" he yelled.

The boys screamed until they were hoarse, but the helicopter showed no sign of noticing them.

A strong beam of light shone out of the belly of the chopper, illuminating the mountain beneath it. As it hovered, from its hatch came a cable, lowering a dark object toward the far side of the mountain.

Tommy gasped as the light caught the object, revealing it to be a large, black metal drum.

"More toxic waste," he called to Hunter. They're dumping more of that nasty stuff."

"I can't believe it," said Hunter.

"Yeah," Tommy muttered. "They're so busy breaking the law, they can't see us. I'm going up there."

"What? Tommy, it's so dark. You'll never make it."

"I have to try. They can't be this close to us and not help us."

"Okay, but take the flashlight and the torch. And be careful!"

Tommy poked the burning torch back into the fire for a few seconds, meanwhile sticking the flashlight into his waistband. Grabbing the torch he hurried up the hill, using the torch to light his path.

With the uneven terrain he stumbled and tripped his way upwards. Once he fell hard, landing on his injured hand. He couldn't stifle the yelp, but that was okay, he thought. Maybe the dumpers would hear him. Not very likely over the noise of their vehicles, but still he hoped.

Scrambling to his feet, he cradled his sore hand even as he held the burning torch in his other one. Gritting his teeth, upward he climbed.

He could hear shouting. Someone was giving directions. The winch that had been lowering the barrels started to reel in as the helicopter slowly rose.

He was so close now. Almost to the top. Surely they would see him.

Then, the chopper was gone. Winch retracted, it whirled and sped off into the blackness. On Tommy climbed. He grunted with every last bit of strength he could muster. The voices of the men on the other side sounded farther away. How had they gotten there? Where had they come from?

No! he thought. Wait, come back! You can't leave yet. He tried to shout, but he had no air. He was panting as he strained to cover the last fifty feet to the top.

He managed a croak. "Wait! Here, help! Come back! Please help us!" He waved the burning torch and screamed.

The men were almost at their vehicle. Did one of them turn back and look? Tommy couldn't be sure. He waved the torch and yelled. Holding the torch between his knees, he whistled through his fingers. He usually could do better than this, but with his throbbing and bandaged hand, it was hard. He yelled and whistled and then waved the branch.

The men climbed into their vehicle, a

camouflage-painted Hum-V, and the diesel-powered vehicle rumbled off into the night.

Tommy stood there at the crest of the mountain, torch in hand. "Wait!" he croaked. "Come back. Please, don't go." Then he crumpled to his knees, sobbing. Pounding the flickering torch on the ground, he wailed until he had no more strength in him.

Part of the branch broke off and tumbled down the hill. It could start a fire, he knew, but he didn't care. Maybe that way someone would find them.

Who was he kidding? Smack out here in the middle of the open desert and still no one could find them. They were going to die, of dehydration, exposure, snakebite, starvation, toxic poisoning – he could take his pick. There were so many choices.

He remembered Hunter, down at the campsite. Dear Hunter, poor kid. His first trip in the desert was a disaster – a fatal disaster. What a waste. He was a smart kid – had a lot of possibilities. Now, he was never going to get to do any of it.

And Tommy himself, he had a few things going for him, too. All wasted.

Well, nothing to be done about it now. They had given it a good shot, but they probably weren't going to make it.

He could hear Hunter calling him. He really should go back to the campsite, but what could he say to Hunter? Nothing. There was nothing he could say. It had been their chance of being rescued and he hadn't been able to pull it off. He hadn't gotten there in time.

Picking himself up off the ground, he started slowly down the mountainside. In the faint glow of moonlight, he picked his way around rocks and cacti. Reaching the fire ring, he plopped down. Again, he sobbed. He couldn't hold back the tears, though he had thought there were none left.

"I – I thought you weren't coming back," Hunter whispered.

Tommy sniffed, shrugged. "What's the use?" he said. He told Hunter how close he had gotten, yet to no avail. He rested his head on his arms propped on his knees.

Both boys were silent for a long time.

Finally Hunter spoke. "So, now what?"

Sniffling, Tommy shrugged. "I don't know. More of the same, I guess."

"Well, I believe what you said last night. I think they're still looking for us. Someone's bound to come by again. We just need to keep doing what we're doing until they find us."

Tommy let out a shaky sigh. "You're right. Guess there's still hope. I just – we were so close. How could they miss me? I was sure that guy turned and looked. But they just left anyway." His voice cracked.

"Maybe they'll tell someone they saw us."

"Yeah, right. They aren't supposed to be here. How can they tell anyone?"

Hunter was silent. "Well, then, maybe some

searchers will find us. You said they're still looking."

Wiping his nose on his sleeve, Tommy said, "You're right. These guys are gone. We need to forget about them and keep doing what we were doing. Someone will find us." His voice was hollow.

"Sure they will."

Tommy scooted over to Spot's cage. "Hey, little guy." He fingered the slats. "Maybe we should let you go, you'd have a better chance."

"No, he wouldn't," said Hunter. "He'd probably use that bad water hole. He's better off with us. We're doing okay. We'll get through this, Tommy. You'll see."

"Yeah," he answered.

"Let's try to get some more sleep. It's four-thirty, almost daylight."

"Right." Tommy stretched out, this time with his head near Spot's cage. Being near the little feline gave him comfort.

Chapter Twenty-four – Another Helicopter

Saturday morning dawned on another bright and sunny day.

"Boy," said Hunter, "a person could almost get tired of this weather. It was never this clear in northern California!"

"Yeah, I guess we are kind of spoiled." The sunshine brought a little cheer to Tommy's mood, but only a little. He still felt heavy and weary from last night's disheartening experience.

This must be what depression feels like, he thought. It's not like me. I'm usually the up-beat one. Well, all we can do is keep going, until we have nothing left.

He let Spot out of his cage on his leash to go to the bathroom. He loved animals so much. Those stupid creeps who were dumping here were killing precious creatures. All the more reason they had to get rescued so they could report it and put an end to it. His determination resurged.

After a breakfast of more cactus fruit and Gatorade water, the boys were in the process of discussing how to build a box trap to catch some mice or squirrels, when the deafening sound of military jets roared overhead.

Both boys jumped! The sound was so loud it almost broke their eardrums.

"The mirror!" Hunter shouted.

Tommy was already on it. He yanked out the mirror and began flashing it in the sunlight.

"Where did they go?" he yelled.

"They went that way!" Hunter pointed northwest after the jets that had already disappeared.

"Oh, please, oh, please! They have to come back." Tommy prayed.

"Flash along the flight path. Maybe there will be more of them. Or maybe they'll come by again. They must be flying training missions."

Tommy turned so that he was reflecting the light along what appeared to be the flight path. He flashed for five minutes though there was nothing in sight.

Then there were planes again. Three in formation, coming from the southeast, heading northwest, like the other ones. The ear-splitting roar shook the ground.

Tommy blinked the light furiously at the jets.

Dot, dot, dot, dash, dash, dash, dot, dot, dot, he signaled. Pause. Dot, dot, dot again. But the planes were already gone.

"Do you think they saw us?" Hunter asked.

"I don't know." Tommy shrugged.

Both boys were sweating and breathing heavily. They collapsed on the hillside by their fire ring. It was possible they had been spotted, but there was no way for them to know. How long would it take for help to come if they had been seen? All they could do was carry on with their activities and be ready if more planes flew over.

They began a project of building a box trap to catch small animals for food. Tommy hated the thought of killing something to eat, but they would starve to death otherwise, and they had Spot to think of, too. The kitten's mother should be providing him food – that was their job now. At least it gave him something to do.

Tommy cut the sticks from a creosote bush and Hunter tied them together with string from his pocket. They built it in the shape of a log cabin, with sticks along the top as well. Then, they selected a spot a short distance from their camp and set up the box. With the open side down, they propped up the opening with a short stick that had a piece of their twine tied to it. All they needed now was bait, and prey.

"So, what do these animals eat?" Hunter asked. "Are they herbivores?"

"Yes, mostly they eat vegetation, maybe some insects. Let's try using those seeds left over from the saguaro fruit and some young leaves from a creosote. Maybe they will like the flower petals and the fuzzy fruit from the creosote, too. Guess we'll just have to try it and see."

About the time the boys had their trap set up, they heard the sound of another helicopter, its wings beating a heavy rhythm. A green military chopper was approaching quickly from the southeast.

Tommy grabbed the mirror and began signaling again. Hunter struggled to his feet and waved his arms wildly. The helicopter slowed and descended, hovering over the plain a short distance from the boys.

"They found us! They found us!" Shouting and waving, the two boys danced around, with Hunter hanging on to Tommy.

The helicopter set down and cut its motor. As the rotor slowed, a sheriff's sergeant jumped from the machine and ran to the boys.

"Well, well, well, are we happy to see you boys! We really had almost given up on you, but the ranger insisted that Tommy – which one of you is Tommy? Anyway, that Tommy would have found a way to survive. And it looks like he was right! And the two of you are together. That's wonderful! We weren't sure if we were searching for one or two of you."

The boys hugged each other and the sergeant as another deputy joined them.

"So, are you boys ready to leave?" the sergeant asked.

"Uh, yeah, we think so, don't we, Hunter?"

"Yeah, okay, but I really was getting to like it here. We were doing all right."

"It sure looks like it," the sergeant confirmed. "You could probably both stand a bath, but otherwise you don't look too much the worse for the wear. Well, except for the leg. What happened?"

"Fell down a mine shaft," Hunter replied sheepishly.

"Oh, and we have a bobcat kitten," Tommy exclaimed. "He's here in this crate. He's okay, I think, except for his leg. He hurt it when we fell down the mine shaft."

The sergeant stooped to peer at the kitten. "Well, look at you," he murmured.

"And we think we know what's the matter with the bobcats," Tommy continued. "Somebody's dumping toxic waste – in this tunnel and over the hill there." He motioned behind them.

"Yeah, they made a drop just last night," Hunter chimed in. "We thought they were going to rescue us, but they just left."

"Really?" said the sergeant. "We'll have to check into that. But, there's plenty of time for all this. Let's get you out of here and radio to your families that you are safe and well."

"Sounds good," the boys said in unison.

Tommy put Hunter's arm over his shoulder and helped him to the helicopter. Several search and rescue personnel packed up Spot and the boys' supplies and loaded them into the chopper.

"A helicopter ride, how cool!" Tommy exclaimed.

"Yeah," Hunter agreed. "My first one ever."

Chapter Twenty-five - Reunion

Later that evening, Tommy and Hunter were sharing a room in the Hidden Wells Community Hospital. Doctors had checked the condition of the boys and found it to be surprisingly good. Hunter's hairline fracture of the tibia was healing well and the makeshift splint had been replaced by a fiberglass cast. Tommy's hand, which was only badly bruised, was in a similar fiberglass wrap for safe-keeping.

The boys were a bit undernourished and only a little dehydrated, but after a day or so in the hospital with rest, fluids and food, they were expected to be just fine. Spot had been delivered to Dr. Martinez at the vet clinic, where he was recovering from surgery on his fractured foreleg.

All of the trip participants and their families

had gathered in the boys' hospital room. Ranger Peterson stepped forward and handed Tommy and Hunter each a certificate. He smiled broadly as he declared,

"Tommy Wilson and Hunter Davidson, you are hereby awarded the grade of A+ for the Summer Ranger Intern Backpacking Trip, for effort and participation above and beyond the call of duty, and for surviving against all odds!" With a flourish, he plopped a Game and Fish Department ball cap on each of the boy's heads.

Everyone in the room applauded and cheered.

Hunter's sunburned face crinkled as he grinned. "I wouldn't have made it without Tommy. It was his expertise that got us through."

Tommy answered. "I wouldn't have made it without Hunter. I may have had the expertise, but there were lots of times when his determination kept me going. I think we worked pretty well together as a team."

The two boys grinned at each other.

Peterson cleared his throat. "Matt and Andy, I spoke with all the parents earlier and they agree that you need to apologize to Tommy and Hunter and their families for your irresponsible, mean, and downright dangerous actions. Who wants to go first?

Andy glanced at Matt, who was staring at the floor. Shifting uncomfortably, Andy wiped his hands on his jeans and spoke.

"I guess I will." He paused, clearing his

throat. Not looking anyone in the eye, he continued, "We, that is Matt thought it would be kind of funny to play a joke on Hunter, since he was new and didn't know the desert very well. We didn't mean for anyone to get hurt."

After a heavy silence in the room, Ranger Peterson said to Andy, "So, it wasn't your idea, but you went along with it, didn't you?"

Andy's head snapped up. His eyes were wide. "Well, yeah, but –" he stammered. Then his face flushed bright red and he hung his head. "Yes," he admitted.

"Was that the spirit of cooperation, teamwork and following of safety rules that we had agreed on?" Peterson asked.

Andy mumbled a barely audible, "No." Then he said, "I'm sorry. I'm so sorry." He looked pleadingly at Hunter and Tommy.

Peterson turned his attention to Matt, who looked ready to bolt from the room.

"Matt, what do you have to say?"

Now, it was the other boy's turn to blush. His jaw was set. "It's like Andy said. It was just supposed to be a joke. No one was supposed to get lost or hurt. That was Hunter's own fault!"

Hunter blinked in surprise and Tommy's jaw hung open. He had expected, at least hoped, that Matt would feel sorry, too.

Peterson pressed Matt for more. "Who sent Hunter off on a wild goose chase in the middle of the night?"

"But, it was just a joke!" Matt insisted.

"No one's laughing, Matt," Peterson said flatly.

"I still say we didn't mean anything by it."

"Yes, you did. You at least meant to embarrass and have fun at someone else's expense. That's not the kind of behavior I want from someone on my expeditions."

Without waiting for any further response, Peterson continued, "In our parents' meeting earlier today, we all decided that a reasonable penalty for Matt's and Andy's actions would be for them to participate in a one-week desert survival course conducted by Outbound Adventures. I pulled some strings and they'll leave on Monday."

Matt stared at the ranger, then at his parents whose faces were sober. "Okay, I'm sorry," he said. "I guess I was trying to make fun of Hunter and that wasn't very nice."

"I'm glad you realize that, Matt," said Peterson. "On this one-week course, you'll get a feel for what you put Hunter and Tommy through, and I hope you'll never do that sort of thing again – either of you."

Peterson continued, "Tommy and Hunter, thanks to you, we now know what we're up against with the bobcats. We've located the toxic canisters and we've launched an all-out search for the culprits based on the details you gave us. When we find them, we're going to throw the book at them." His tanned face was grim.

"Good!" said Tommy and Hunter together.

Tommy held up his injured hand and smiled,

"At least I can still work at the clinic and take care of the animals with one hand."

"Yeah, and I can't wait to see the clinic," said Hunter.

The ranger's cell phone rang. He answered and listened to the caller. "Hey, that's great to hear. I'll tell the boys."

Disconnecting the call, he announced, "That was the office. A man called in and reported seeing you boys last night. He admitted to the toxic dumping and agreed to testify against his employer. It's an outfit we've been trying to nail for months."

"All right!" cheered Tommy and Hunter.

The group gathered around to listen as the boys recounted their adventures, describing how the Air Force jets had seen their mirror signal and then the sheriff's helicopter had located them from the marker they had made.

When everyone wanted to sign his cast, Hunter insisted that Tommy be the first.

Tommy said, "Even though there were some tough times, I think we had a successful expedition. I'd go again, but only if Hunter goes, too. Next time, though, let's stay away from old mine shafts," he finished with a grin.

Desert Survival Checklist

Water – carry as much as you can!

- ☐ gloves
- ☐ maps
- ☐ signal mirror
- ☐ police whistle
- ☐ butane lighter
- ☐ waterproof case w/matches
- ☐ first aid kit
- ☐ needle & thread
- ☐ pencil & paper
- ☐ pocket knife
- ☐ flashlight
- ☐ energy bars
- ☐ dried fruit & nuts
- ☐ large garbage bags
- ☐ clear plastic bags
- ☐ sun hat
- ☐ sunglasses
- ☐ sunblock lotion
- ☐ jacket & long pants
- ☐ sturdy boots
- ☐ nylon cord
- ☐ insect repellent

Desert Survival Tips

- Always "file a flight plan" – tell someone where you're going and when you'll be back
- Drink as much as you can
- If you get lost, stay in one place
- Take shelter from the sun, heat, and weather
- Drink as much as you can
- Work on getting rescued – help them find you with fires, signals and markers
- Drink as much as you can

Bobcat Fact Sheet
Felis Rufus

- A bobcat's coat is reddish or brown with lighter color on the underbody and patterns of dark stripes or spots.
- The bobcat gets its name from its short, "bobbed" tail, which has black on the tip.
- Also characteristic are the black tufts of fur on each ear, which gives the bobcat acute hearing.
- Bobcats also have dense fur on their cheeks, forming tufts.
- Bobcats are nocturnal, though they may be active also in daytime.
- They are carnivores.
- Adult bobcats weigh between 10 and 25 pounds; with males weighing more than females.
- Bobcats are found in a wide range of habitats, from forests to grasslands to semiarid deserts.
- Bobcats mate in late winter or early spring and have litters of 2-4 kittens in about 60 days.
- The kittens stay with the mother for almost a year, while she teaches them to hunt and survive.

Maggie Caldwell Smith's childhood years were spent growing up in California and Arizona, always on the deserts. Even when she was young, the desert and its surprising wealth in the face of apparent barrenness intrigued her. She has spent time living in many parts of the world, from southern California to Arizona, to Finland, England and Germany, with extensive visits in most western European countries and even a short visit to Kenya and Uganda in East Africa.

Maggie loves words and working and playing with them. Through the years she has studied Russian, French, Spanish, Finnish, Swedish and German. She discovered early her love for communication, as evidenced by her father's nickname for her: Magpie. When not writing and researching her books, Maggie substitute teaches. She lives with her husband in Pine Mountain Club, California.